# SCENES OF CRIME

## As Dell Shannon

CASE PENDING
THE ACE OF SPADES
EXTRA KILL
KNAVE OF HEARTS
DEATH OF A BUSYBODY
DOUBLE BLUFF
ROOT OF ALL EVIL
MARK OF MURDER
THE DEATH-BRINGERS
DEATH BY INCHES
COFFIN CORNER
WITH A VENGEANCE
CHANCE TO KILL
RAIN WITH VIOLENCE
SCHOOLED TO KILL
KILL WITH KINDNESS
CRIME ON THEIR HANDS
UNEXPECTED DEATH
WHIM TO KILL
THE RINGER
MURDER WITH LOVE
WITH INTENT TO KILL
NO HOLIDAY FOR CRIME
SPRING OF VIOLENCE
CRIME FILE
DEUCES WILD

## As Elizabeth Linington

THE PROUD MAN

THE LONG WATCH
MONSIEUR JANVIER
THE KINGBREAKER
POLICEMAN'S LOT
ELIZABETH I (Encyclopedia Brittanica)
GREENMASK!
NO EVIL ANGEL
DATE WITH DEATH
SOMETHING WRONG
PRACTISE TO DECEIVE
CRIME BY CHANCE

## As Egan O'Neill

THE ANGLOPHILE

## As Lesley Egan

A CASE FOR APPEAL
THE BORROWED ALIBI
AGAINST THE EVIDENCE
RUNT TO EVIL
MY NAME IS DEATH
DETECTIVE'S DUE
A SERIOUS INVESTIGATION
THE WINE OF VIOLENCE
IN THE DEATH OF A MAN
MALICIOUS MISCHIEF
PAPER CHASE

# SCENES OF CRIME

LESLEY EGAN

PUBLISHED FOR THE CRIME CLUB BY
DOUBLEDAY & COMPANY, INC.
GARDEN CITY, NEW YORK
1976

All of the characters in this book
are fictitious, and any resemblance
to actual persons, living or dead,
is purely coincidental.

Library of Congress Cataloging in Publication Data

Linington, Elizabeth.
    Scenes of crime.

    I. Title.
PZ4.L756Sb [PS3562.I515]    813'.5'4

*First Edition*

ISBN: 0-385-11468-0
Library of Congress Catalog Card Number 75-36590
Copyright © 1976 by Elizabeth Linington
All Rights Reserved
Printed in the United States of America

If this world were good for nothing else, it is a fine subject for speculation.

—*William Hazlitt*

What a world of gammon and spinnage it is, though, ain't it?

—DAVID COPPERFIELD, *Charles Dickens*

# SCENES OF CRIME

# ONE

O'Connor toiled up the steep slope, panting. He reflected ruefully that he'd been known in former days as a chaser of females,
but he'd never expected to be chasing this kind of female over
such terrain. He stopped to get his breath and shouted after
her. "Maisie, girl, not so fast!"

She galloped back and, rising up at him lovingly, nearly
knocked him over. "I had to fall for one like you," said O'Connor exasperatedly, and she waved her feather-duster tail at
him pleasedly. She was outsize even for an Afghan hound, and
her silver-blue coat shone in the warm June sun. Officially she
was registered as Nefer-Mayet-Yti of Sakkara, but even at fifteen
months she was not a dignified dog, and for some time had
answered to the nickname. Well, Katy had warned him, thought
O'Connor, getting out a cigarette. Running up mountains after
his blue girl, seeing she got enough exercise; but he wasn't going
to run any farther today. The usual June heat wave was building up, and already a faint haze obscured the view over the
city from this thickly brushed hill above Glendale College.

O'Connor sat down on a convenient flat boulder and relaxed; it had been a pull up the hill, from the nearest street
nearly a mile below. It was past ten o'clock; let Maisie have another good run up here, and get on home to take Katy out to the
late Sunday brunch at Pike's Verdugo Oaks. O'Connor sat
thinking fondly and fatuously of Katy and the baby due in
November, finished the cigarette and lit another, and looked
around for his blue girl. She had vanished.

With those long legs she could be over the county line when
his back was turned. Resignedly O'Connor got up and started up

the hill through wild sumac and thick-growing yellow mustard. "Maisie!" Somewhere ahead of him she barked sharply. He called again and spotted the tip of an agitated tail off to his right, where a lone scrub-oak stood. "Maisie, girl—time to go home. Come on." Her second bark was urgent; she was nosing at something there. O'Connor got tangled in a tall sumac bush and swore. "What've you found now? Come on—" Apt to be anything from an empty bird's nest to beer cans—but after a careless glance O'Connor halted and stared. "*Heel!*" he said roughly, and recognizing that he meant it for once, Maisie backed up and sat down meekly.

"My good God in Heaven!" said O'Connor, and made the instant transition from dog owner to lieutenant of police. And the nearest phone was a mile down the hill—but at least there wasn't going to be a crowd around to disturb the evidence. He wheeled and started back down, with Maisie following reluctantly.

A hundred yards from where he'd left the Ford was a house, one of the few new homes yet built in this newest subdivision. O'Connor snapped Maisie's leash on and marched up to push the bell. By the time the door was opened he had the badge out. "Sorry to disturb you, but I'd like to use your phone. Lieutenant O'Connor, Glendale Police."

The householder was a burly, big fellow evidently just out of bed, a bathrobe over striped pajamas; he stared at O'Connor uncomprehendingly. "Police? What's wrong?"

"I just want to use your phone, please, sir."

"Well, sure, but what's going on?" He peered out to the empty street. "Oh, sure—it's in the den, right here—my wife's not up yet—is anything wrong?"

"Thanks very much, sir," said O'Connor, and firmly shut the door on him. Dialing automatically, he got Sergeant Duff at the desk and said tersely, "Me. Who's in?"

"Everybody but John and Fred, why? We just had a heist. It's your day off."

"Like hell," said O'Connor. "Varallo there? Gimme . . .

Vic? I just found a thing, that is Maisie did. Bodies. Looks like the hell of a thing, whatever. You'd better get up here with Burt and Thomsen—and get hold of Goulding if you can. I think he'd better have a look before we move 'em. And an ambulance."

"Bodies?" said Varallo incredulously. "Plural? Where, for God's sake?"

"About a mile above Parkmount Drive—up the hill. Plural is right. They're kids, Vic—little kids, looks like three. And they've been here awhile."

"*Dio!*" said Varallo. "All right, we'll be there."

O'Connor put the phone down and then picked it up again and dialed the house on Virginia Avenue. Better tell Katy he wouldn't be home to take her to lunch. But no details—not a good idea to tell her horror stories . . .

"For heaven's sake, Charles," said Katharine, "I'm not about to have a miscarriage because you tell me there's a new homicide. So you found a body and you won't be home for a while. I'll be seeing it in the paper, I suppose, whether you tell me the details or not."

"Now, Katy—it's just that you can't be too careful—"

"Honestly, men. All right, darling, I'll see if Laura wants to go with me."

Varallo, Burt, and Thomsen got up there to park behind O'Connor's Ford half an hour later, and Dr. Goulding's old Caddy was a minute behind them; Varallo had got him at home. O'Connor was waiting up beyond the house to point the way. The householders were peering interestedly out the front door. "What the hell, Lieutenant—kids?" said Burt. "Dead?"

"But very. You'd better save your breath for the climb." By the time they were fifty yards up the hill, laden with the lab kit and camera, Burt and Thomsen were puffing. The cadaverous Goulding stalked behind silently. O'Connor had left Maisie tied to the car, and she called after them as long as she could see them.

"I thought you'd better have a look before we did any poking around, Doctor," O'Connor said as they came up to the scrub-oak. "Give us some idea about the time—ages—whatever." The others exclaimed, looking at the horrid, pathetic tangle at the foot of the tree, and Burt set the lab kit down with a little thud. "Jesus," he said. Varallo just took a long breath. Goulding offered no immediate comment.

The two uppermost bodies lay one half on top of the other: shrunken, wizened little bodies, the ugly staining of death on bare arms and legs: a few shreds of clothes. There was a much smaller body almost hidden beneath those, one tiny arm looking like a wooden doll's arm thrust out stiffly. "*Cristo*," said Varallo softly. "Why haven't they been found before, Charles? Right out in the open, and not all that far from civilization."

"Far enough," said O'Connor. "No hiking trails or bike trails up here. Not very convenient for neckers or picnics. I was up here with the dog for the first time last week, but further over toward the college. What about it, Doctor?"

Goulding grunted and went to kneel beside the little heap. His bald head shone nakedly in the sun. There wasn't any real need, on a force the size of Glendale's, for a full-time police surgeon; but Goulding, coming into some money a few years before, had gratefully resigned from private practice with all its red tape and paperwork, and retired to his cubbyhole of an office in the jail, pottering around the lab when there wasn't any medical work to do. Police work had always fascinated him; one of his axioms was that doctors and detectives had a lot in common.

"I'd only be guessing," he said now. "Poor little bastards. Couple of months maybe—maybe not that long. But it's been dry and warm, it could be longer. Just luck the coyotes don't range down this far in summer. Whatever we find out 'll be in the lab, Charles. You'll want pictures before we move them." He stood up and Burt got out the camera.

"But, my God, just kids!" said Thomsen. "Can't tell if they're boys or girls, but they can't be over three or four—my God, what's happening to people these days?"

It was a question cops asked lately. It did make you wonder, thought Varallo. Kids, any kids, ought to have people to love and cherish them: be concerned about them. "There hasn't been anything like this on the missing list—three kids all together."

"Not on ours," said O'Connor. "We'll be asking around." Burt had got pictures from several angles, and the doctor was gently moving the bodies now, separating them, straightening them out on the ground. "We'd better have a good look around here for any scrap of evidence. Christ, what a thing." Some of the mess and dirt and blood cops got used to, after a fashion; but this kind of thing, never. And Varallo was thinking inevitably of his darling Ginevra at home, plump and blond and cosseted—and the new one to come in November; as he supposed O'Connor was thinking of his Katy and the baby. And he thought what he'd just said: not so far from civilization? This was about as far from that as you could get.

"Get them down to the morgue and I'll have a better look," said Goulding. "Provisionally, I'll say two boys, about four and two, and a baby—probably under a year. Hard to say whether any of the staining is ante mortem or not. There's been some cutting."

Varallo ran a hand through his tawny crest of hair and said absently, "Quiet Sunday until this showed up. We had a funny sort of heist just before you called in, Charles. A pair of females. With a baby."

"You don't say," said O'Connor. "World going to hell, Vic. Something happening to people. Aughh! I don't know, maybe we're a pair of damned fools, bringing more innocent kids into it."

"Well, the girls don't think so. There come the ambulance boys."

And— "Oh, hell!" said O'Connor—Maisie had chewed herself loose from the car and came galloping after them joyously up the hill, ears and topknot flying. "You mean the heisters were female? With a baby? On Sunday morning?"

"At a discount market out on Glenoaks," said Varallo.

"Listen, I was so *surprised*," said the market checker, "who was noticing the color eyes they had or what they had on, I ask you? With a gun on me, I'm noticing clothes?" Her name was Marion Nealy, she was fat and forthright and indignant, and she chewed gum faster and faster as she talked, telling Poor and Wayne all about it for the third time. "They came up to the counter together with a basket, and I'm starting to check the stuff out, and all of a sudden one of them pulls a gun out of her purse and says to hand over the money—and who notices what customers look like, up to then they were just customers, mister—"

"Sergeant," said Wayne. "Could you give us any idea of their ages?"

"Gee, I don't know—kind of young, I guess."

The market manager came bustling up with another female. The market had only just opened when the heisters had appeared, and the first squad car had got here before any other customers came in; a little knot of them was waiting now outside the locked doors, but in here were only three checkers and the manager, Al Lorenzo. "Margie thinks she can describe them, Sergeant—I was in the office like I said, but Margie saw them —this is Margie Hogan, Sergeant—"

"I sure did," said Margie, who was small and redheaded and excited. "And what's more, I think I'd seen one of them before. The one with the baby. I waited on her once, I'm positive. They were here when we opened up—when Mr. Lorenzo unlocked the doors at ten-thirty. They came right in, there wasn't another customer in, and I was checking my change and they went past my counter up past table three like they were after cigarettes or candy along there—"

"So all right," said Poor. "What did they look like?"

"One of 'em's got dark brown hair, she's about, oh, couple of inches taller than me, maybe twenty-six, twenty-seven, and she's thin. The other one—the one with the baby—she's younger and blond and a little bit taller. They both had jeans and blouses on, light-colored, I think, but that's all I could say—"

"And nobody saw them get into a car outside?"

They all shook their heads. "I didn't see any of it, I was in the office," said Lorenzo.

"Listen, I was so *shook*," said Marion Nealy, "they coulda took off in a balloon, mister! I handed over the money—look, all the prices now and all the big bills around, we get two hundred fifty in paper and fifty in change, just to start out. That's what they got, see—most of the change was still in rolls, I hadn't put it in the register yet, and one of 'em just grabbed it and stuck it in her bag and they went out the nearest door—that one there —and then I sort of came to and yelled for Mr. Lorenzo, and Margie came over—"

Poor looked at Wayne and sighed. As usual, the market was on a corner and had a huge parking lot in front. The two heisters could have walked quietly around the corner of the building, climbed into a car parked on the street, and mingled with traffic out there on Glenoaks Boulevard in two minutes. "Could you tell us anything about the gun?" asked Poor. "Big, little— revolver, automatic?"

Marion just shrugged. "It was a gun, that's all. Black, and I guess not very big. But am I gonna ask questions, with a gun on me?"

"Oh, the baby," said Margie. "It's crazy, isn't it, holding up a place with a baby?" She was eying Fred Wayne with frank admiration, his size and evident muscles. "I think it's a girl, Sergeant—an awfully cute baby, with a lot of curly blond hair, and it had on a little blue knit jumpsuit. I mean, they looked ordinary—just a couple of women with a baby—it's crazy, isn't it?"

"Crazy is not the word," said Lorenzo gloomily. "A liquor store I used to have, my own store—and I get fed up with all the paperwork and taxes and keeping decent help, but mostly I get fed up with the heists—six times I got heisted in the last year, and I get fed up, I take this nice quiet job here, no sweat, so now I'm getting heisted by females! Not to mention all the shoplifting. I tell you, I've got a mind to get out of the big town and go back to Marysville. Out of the rat race. My God, female heisters."

There wasn't anything Poor and Wayne could do about it; one thing Marion was sure of, neither of the women had touched the counter, so it'd be no use dusting for possible prints. They asked the two girls to come in and make statements, and drove back to headquarters. Joe Katz was typing a report at his desk; Jeff Forbes's lanky length was sprawled at his as he read a paperback. He looked up as they came in.

"Something new gone down, boys. The lieutenant called in just after you went out—he's found some bodies up in the wilds when he was walking that dog."

"Bodies—plural? Business picking up," said Wayne. "What a way to make a living."

Laura had left Ginevra under the grandmotherly eye of Mrs. Anderson next door and met Katharine up at Pike's Verdugo Oaks. They lingered over a rather lavish lunch; after all, as Katharine said, helping herself to shrimp Louis, they were eating for two. And perhaps it wasn't such a funny coincidence, both babies due in November, seeing that they were both married to the dedicated cops.

"But Charles is maddening—you'd think I was made of glass, and I never felt better in my life. I'm dying to hear all about the body up there, and I don't suppose he'll tell me a thing, so mind you get it all out of Vic."

"Men," said Laura, munching cheese toast, "are always fairly maddening. It's only fair I should name this one, and Vic's raising an awful fuss about it. Because—well, I think backgrounds are important. You know? You ought to be proud of what you are, of your name, whether it's Italian or French or Irish or whatever—and it wouldn't matter so much about a girl, but if it's a boy he'll stay Varallo all his life and I think he ought to have a name to match. I'd like to name him for Vic— but he's absolutely put his foot down and says he wouldn't saddle a dog with a name like Lodovico Giovanni—"

"Yes, well, it is rather a mouthful," said Katharine, buttering another roll.

"So I said what about Stevano and we could call him Steve— or Arturo and we'd call him Art—though I would really love to name him Lodovico and call him Lodo—it'd be cute," said Laura, "But Vic said over his dead body and if it's a boy it'll be John. Period. And it's so *tame*."

"Charles doesn't care, luckily. Whatever I decide, except not a junior. But you know the funny thought I had, Laura—"

"I know." Laura nodded her bright brown head, surveying Katharine and again absently envying her tall, dark elegance. "I had it too. Wouldn't it be funny if one of us had a girl and the other a boy and they grew up and got married?"

"Funnier things have happened," said Katharine. "I'm going back for some more shrimp. But that at least is one good thing. Poor Charles—"

"What?"

"It always annoys him so that I can eat like a horse and never gain a pound. But just as I predicted, chasing after that dog is helping to keep his weight down. I suppose it was Maisie found the body, come to think."

"I can only thank heaven," said Laura. "that Vic's gone in for roses as a hobby. That dog."

"It's like those signs," said Katharine. "You know, that say *All valuables marked for identification*, whether they really are or not. The theory being that the burglar won't take the chance they are. That's Maisie. She's so big and loud, we just hope no burglar would come through the gate to find out she loves the world and everybody in it. If Charles had only fallen for a Peke—or even a fox terrier. Do you want that last roll?"

"No, thanks—I'm going back for some more potato salad."

O'Connor, Varallo, Burt, and Thomsen had just got back to headquarters—none of them had wanted any lunch—and were telling Poor, Katz, and Wayne about the bodies, when Sergeant Duff buzzed the detective office.

"You've got a rape to work now."

"Oh, for God's sake," said O'Connor, who had picked up the phone. "For real, statutory, or what?"

"Somebody can go and find out—I don't know. A Dr. Muller just called in from the Memorial. Girl by the name of Stephanie Calvert was brought into emergency about 4 A.M. She's just come to—been beaten up, so it sounds like a for-real assault."

"All right, all right." O'Connor put the phone down and re-layed that. "One of you can go question her. It's my day off, I'm going home."

Wayne said he hadn't finished the report on the heist. Varallo should be starting a preliminary report on the bodies, not that there'd be much in it; they'd bloodhounded over the ground up there without finding anything that might be evidence tied up to the bodies. Katz was still busy over a follow-up report on the liquor-store heist last week. As usual, there were odds and ends to clear up: still on the books to work were that, a hit-run with one D.O.A. and no leads, and a somewhat monumental job of vandalism on a brand-new office building over on Arden Avenue, windows smashed, floors ripped up, wall paneling demolished, and no leads on that either. They were still trying to find a name for the body found on the street on South Brand a week ago; nobody around here had his prints on file, and they were waiting to hear if the FBI had them—just another derelict dead of drink, but if there was any family they could pay for a funeral. There was an inquest pending on last Wednesday's suicide.

"You'd better go look at the rape, Vic," said Katz, yawning.

"She won't be thinking much of men at the moment and maybe our handsome blond Eytie cop will reassure her."

Varallo said he doubted it, but somebody had to go, so he did. And it was a little thing maybe, but he did resent that arbitrarily high parking fee at the Memorial Hospital lot; he drove the Gremlin around several blocks before he found a slot on the street.

Upstairs in Emergency, he talked to Dr. Muller, who was young and dispassionate. "She's been knocked around and half strangled as well as raped. Concussion, but she seems to be a strong, healthy girl with a lot of common sense, and I wouldn't expect any trauma. Yes, you can talk to her, but not too long— I expect you'll have seen the police report, she managed to call them and they got the ambulance, about three-fifty this morning." Varallo hadn't seen it; the night watch reports would just be drifting in now.

Stephanie Calvert was a good-looking young woman in a big, wholesome, country-girl way, with a lot of light brown hair and a wide mouth made for smiling. Right now she was pale, a little drowsy under sedation, and there was a large, discolored bruise on one cheek, bruises on her throat. She looked up at Varallo hazily.

"They always say—invited it—but I didn't," she murmured, squinting at the badge. "Really. Don't even—date much." From what the hospital had, he knew she worked at the Bank of America as a teller, lived alone in an apartment on Stocker. "Didn't go out—last night. Washed my hair and went to bed— after I finished a letter to Mother. Oh, my God, I hope you haven't called her—she'd have a *fit*. She didn't want me to move—to the big city anyway. All I know, I woke up—heard him getting in, I suppose—and next thing he was just *there*. Trying to strangle me—"

"Just take it easy, Miss Calvert. I realize it was dark, but can you give me any idea what he looked like? Age—height— clothes?"

She shook her head slightly and winced. "Dark—it sure was— and I'd waked up all of a sudden—hands on my throat. He was strong. Young, I think—I don't know. But—it was crazy. Just crazy. He whispered to me—he said it over and over— 'Remember Maggie Walters!' I think that was it—no sense—and then he—"

Varallo said, "I will be damned. I really will be—. You're sure of that?" And that was about all she was sure of: and more than enough. Maggie Walters. That opened up wide that old case shoved in Pending last February. As he rode down in the elevator he was trying to remember all the details. Two rapes, break-ins at a house, apartment?—and both women saying the rapist had whispered that to them. Remember Maggie Walters. Why? Who was she? They had done all the indicated detective work then, but nothing had showed. Now here he was again.

When he got back to the office. O'Connor was still there. Since he had been married, Katharine's civilizing effect had somewhat toned down his language, but when he heard what Varallo had to say he came out with a few choice expletives. Even respectably dressed in suit and white shirt O'Connor always looked the complete tough; on his day off, simply clad in old slacks and a sweat shirt, muscles bulging, at this time of day his chin blue with heavy beard, his black hair curling with perspiration, he looked like a gangster in a 1930s movie. "That thing!" he said. "Jesus H. Christ, that thing! We thought we had a little lead on it—not worth a damn really—those gloves found at the scene, but the lab couldn't turn anything. There wasn't a smell—and now you tell me we've got another? To do all the goddamned paperwork on and get nowhere?"

"Well, it is a felony," said Varallo mildly. "She seems like a nice girl, Charles."

"So go and start the routine!" said O'Connor. "It's still my day off." He stood up and then regarded Varallo seriously, fingering his heavy blue jaw. "You know something? Not that I claim any ESP—but I've got a hunch, just what's gone down today—we're in for a spate of funny ones. They come along. Human nature or whatever. The peculiar ones—the offbeat ones. Those kids—oh hell, I'm going home."

"Don't borrow trouble, *amico*," said Varallo. But the funny ones did come along; once in a while there was a little run of them. He just hoped O'Connor's ESP was on the wrong track.

He collected Burt from the lab and they went over to Stephanie Calvert's apartment on Stocker. It would probably be a futile gesture, but they'd dust surfaces for possible prints and look around for any physical evidence.

The only immediate deduction to be made from the apartment was that X had been quick about getting in: the door had been kicked in, the lock fairly flimsy and lacking a deadbolt. Varallo had a guess that Stephanie would have put up a good fight if she hadn't been taken completely by surprise. As it was, they would have to go through the motions, and be surprised if they turned up any useful prints. This time no glove had been left, if that had meant anything in the first two cases. The professional forcing of the door didn't say anything: too many people had seen too many doors kicked in by police on a lot of TV shows.

Occasionally Varallo wondered academically why he'd ever wanted to go on being a cop. After twelve years on a force upstate, resigning as captain, why he hadn't gone in for insurance, or stockbroking, or clerking in a store, or writing greeting-card verses—anything but being a cop. He supposed it was force of habit that had led him to Glendale Police Headquarters to ask humbly if he could please be a cop again. Talk about thankless jobs—

At four-thirty that Sunday afternoon Patrolman Neil Tracy called into the station and asked for a detective. He got Joe Katz.

"Look," said Tracy, "this is maybe a piddling little thing, but maybe not too, because I find out she's on probation, see. And I just think one of you brain-trust boys ought to know about it, and maybe make a report."

"On what?" asked Katz.

"This Roberta Finch. Teen-ager. If you ask me, she's nuts, but I'm just a simple cop," said Tracy. "She tried to poison a neighbor's dog, and naturally there was a ruckus—they got the dog in time, it's all right, but the neighbor's fit to be tied and I can't say I blame her. And when I ask a few questions, I find out this Finch girl is on probation for assault—there's a new hearing scheduled in juvenile court next month. This could have a bearing on that—I thought I'd better tell somebody."

"You thought right," said Katz. "What's the address?" Before he left the office he consulted their juvenile records, didn't find anything listed under Finch, and swore; but the name hadn't rung any bells and if it had been in their jurisdiction he'd have remembered it, a teen-ager up for assault. He tried the Hollywood division of LAPD and hit lucky the first time. She was in their records. Female aged fifteen years, charged with assault of two juveniles aged two and four left in her charge as baby-sitter. It dated back to March; she'd been put on probation, psychiatric exam ordered, and a new hearing scheduled on the parents' petition.

Funny you could say, thought Katz. Could be the lieutenant was right, they were going to get a run of the peculiar ones. In his own way Joe Katz was something of a philosopher; he reflected now that in police work 99 per cent of what they ran across was the random, reasonless violence, the stupidity and simple greed and irresponsibility—but the other one per cent was sometimes the active ultimate evil. He smelled a little brimstone right now.

Dr. Goulding had made a preliminary examination of the three little bodies; he would get to the first autopsy tonight, the others tomorrow. Like all good surgeons he could be dispassionate about the job, but that didn't mean he was cold-blooded. He seethed with righteous indignation that three small children had been (however) wantonly allowed to die, and with consuming curiosity as to how it had happened. There were a couple of visible wounds; the autopsies would tell them something definite.

He was just leaving his office, having reassured his wife he'd be home for dinner, when the phone shrilled at him.

"Oh, Goulding—ah—I hoped perhaps to get you there. I—ah —wanted to consult you about this case—"

Annoyed, Goulding recognized the voice. Norenberg. A competent physician, a good man, but overconscientious. A worrier. An old maid of a fellow, always fussing over little things, even when they'd gone through pre-med together thirty years ago. "Yes?"

"As consultant to the police, you could advise me—that is, it was quite unexpected, you know, I had confidently expected her to live for years—heart quite sound, blood-pressure excellent, kidneys—there was no indication at all—only the rheumatoid arthritis, and really it was such a surprise to me—I'd like to know for certain, you see. I have asked permission to do an autopsy, and there was a little difficulty, but really I felt—not that I'm suggesting there was—but—

"So the autopsy should tell you something definite. What do you want from me?" asked Goulding.

"I'm not an autopsy surgeon," said Norenberg fretfully. "I haven't done an autopsy in years. I thought if you—"

"Do you suspect homicide?" asked Goulding bluntly.

"Good heavens, no—ridiculous! An old lady of nearly eighty, in a convalescent home—everyone devoted to her. But I don't see any reason she should have popped off like this, and I'd like to know I thought—benefit of your experience—they've already arranged the funeral, it'll have to be done in the morning—"

"What time?" asked Goulding resignedly.

Driving toward home—he'd type a report on it tomorrow, it was end of shift—Katz speculated uneasily on the Finch girl. Brimstone and evil, he thought, for sure. Funny: a nice home, the parents looked like very upright, responsible people. Finch an attorney: two younger kids, boy and girl, looked like nice kids. And that girl: sullen, mostly silent, peering up from half-lidded eyes under an untidy tangle of brown hair. "It barked at me. I don't like it." So she'd coated a couple of cookies with snail poison and thrown them over the wall to the neighbor's little Cocker. Just luck the neighbor had seen her, and come out in time to snatch them away.

Everybody distressed and voluble, except that girl. Nuts, Tracy said. And this was a misdemeanor, she'd have to appear in juvenile court here—the Lord knew when, the calendar was always full; but Katz thought he'd pass it on to Hollywood. Interesting to see what the psychiatrist made of her: not that he put much stock in the doubletalk of the head doctors. The baby-sitter assaulting the kids—trying to poison a dog. Funny-peculiar. Katz thought probably other cops would be concerned with the Finch girl from time to time.

The night watch came on, and up to eight o'clock nothing much showed up; nothing for Detective Dick Hunter, Detective Bob Rhys holding down the detective office. Traffic picked up a couple of drunks and ran a brief high-speed pursuit of a hit-run driver, losing him on the freeway. Sunday night was usually quiet in Glendale.

Rhys had just yawned for the third time and announced he'd be glad to go back on day watch when Sergeant Harrison buzzed him from the desk.

"Heist reported," he said tersely. "That all-night drugstore at the new professional building on Central."

"Well, something to do, anyway," said Rhys. They both went out on it.

At the pharmacy two uniformed men, Stoner and Gordon, were talking to the white-coated elderly man behind the counter. He was only slightly shaken, and could tell them precisely what loot had gone— "I'd only just taken over from Mac, for the night shift, and just finished checking the register. It was a hundred and ninety-six fifty-four. But I couldn't believe my eyes—two women! Ordinary young women—when they came up to the counter I naturally thought, a prescription—I said—and then one of them pulled a gun! I couldn't believe it—"

# TWO

When the day watch drifted in on Monday morning Hunter's report on that was waiting on O'Connor's desk. "I'll be damned, the same pair," he said, shoving it across to Varallo. "Not satisfied with the little loot they got at the market." By the night clerk's description, one brown-haired, medium height, the other taller and blond, that pair—but no baby this time. "Past its bedtime," suggested Varallo. No description of the gun, but the clerk thought one or both of them might have touched the register; they'd come right around the counter to take the money. Rhys had dusted both counter and register and lifted a number of fair latents, but whether any of them belonged to the heisters was something else. It would make a morning's work for Burt, checking them, looking in records.

It was Poor's day off, so they were a man short. Somebody would have to cover the inquest on the suicide. And there was legwork to do on the rape. O'Connor was still illogically annoyed about the rape. In detective work theoretically the more offbeat a thing was the easier it was to solve; in practice that didn't always work out. "Go the same damn route as on the first two," he said, scowling, "and come up with damn all." One thing at least they could skip, Varallo reminded him; on the first two, they'd followed up the Maggie Walters bit, and that had been a dead end. No force anywhere around, or the National Crime Information Center, had any record of a Maggie Walters. Presumably she was important to the rapist, but they'd have to drop on him to find out why.

Yesterday Varallo and Forbes hadn't found anybody at home in the apartment house where Stephanie lived: a warm June

Sunday, not too surprising. They couldn't expect to find many people home today; probably most of the residents had jobs; but they drove up to Stocker in Varallo's little Gremlin to knock on doors—they had to be thorough. It was a new building, two stories and eight apartments. At the right rear on the second floor, they found a harassed Mrs. Thorsen home with a fretful baby, but she couldn't tell them anything. She'd been up with the baby all Saturday night, hadn't heard a thing from the front of the building, hadn't known about the break-in. "We don't know that girl—Miss Calvin, something like that?—goodness, that's terrible, but I never heard a thing and Joe sleeps like a log."

"This is a waste of time," said Forbes.

"You never know when you'll turn something," said Varallo. Nobody else answered doorbells until they tried the one just opposite Stephanie's; Varallo pushed it three times and had just turned away when the door opened a crack.

"Oh—I thought it was the man from the drugstore. There's a sign about no peddling in the building." She was a slim, dark girl, pretty, but obviously suffering a heavy cold, eyes red and swollen, voice thick.

Varallo showed her the badge. "We'd just like to ask a few questions, Miss—"

"Lee," she said. "Oooh, you cops?" She stared from him to Forbes interestedly, brushing back her tangled hair. "Say, I'm sorry—I look a mess, I've got this cold—only reason I'm home. What's it about?" She hadn't known about the break-in either, and was more excited than alarmed. "When did you say it happened?—right across the hall, the Calvert girl—my God! Of all things—oh, wait till Sandra hears—Sandra and I share this place, that's Sandra Hoffman—I'm Jeanie Lee. But we didn't—did you say *Saturday* night, after midnight, I mean, that'd be Sunday morn—Oh, my goodness! Oh, my goodness, I wonder if that was *him!*" She clutched her throat in unconscious dramatic gesture.

"Who?" asked Forbes.

"Oh, my goodness! Just wait till Sandra hears! Maybe you'd

better come in—excuse the way the place looks. I've been feeling so lousy—just sit anywhere. I shouldn't have gone out Saturday at all, I was coming down with this damned cold, but we'd had the date set up for a week, see. With Bob and Chris—nice guys—Bob had tickets for this preview movie house over in Hollywood, and then we went to a disco somewhere and danced —oh, I don't suppose you're interested in that—" She'd settled most of her attention on Varallo. "Anyway, it was late when the boys dropped us outside—it was after three—and just as we came in, this fellow was coming down the stairs. It was funny—queer, I mean, we said so then, because the Thorsens never have parties, that's the right rear, and the left rear's old Miss Thatcher, she's seventy if she's a day and goes to bed about nine o'clock—and we said, it just showed you—"

"Showed you what?" asked Varallo patiently.

"Well, if it was *him*, of course it didn't—it wasn't, I mean. But that Calvert girl's so damned strait-laced, see—we asked her to Sandra's birthday party and she wouldn't even take a drink, and she acted so prissy when Bob told a couple of stories, not really dirty but you know—and here was this fellow sneaking out of her apartment at three-thirty A.M., I mean it was the only place he could've come from—and we said—"

"Could you tell us what he looked like, Miss Lee?"

"Well, goodness, I don't know," she said blankly. "He was in a hurry, he came running down the stairs and went straight out —it was just a fellow, that's all. Sort of young, medium-sized— he had his head down, and he kind of ducked down—that was another thing made us think—he hadn't expected to see us, and he was getting out in a hurry, and we thought—but if he was the *one!* Broke in and assaulted—oh, my goodness! Well, maybe Sandra could tell you more, I don't think so, but just imagine, us just walking in and seeing him—it's a wonder he didn't do something to us! Oh, wait till Sandra—"

Sandra, it appeared, worked at Sears, in Customer Service. They spent half an hour talking to her, and she was just as surprised and excited as Jeanie but couldn't add anything to the description. "But it adds up to a little break," said Varallo on the way back to headquarters. "Because the time fits—that had to be X on his way out—and if it is a very general description, at least it weeds out any possibles who are over five-ten, or fat. Which helps some."

"It's the way we usually do it." And they had done it before on the first two cases: started looking for the sex offenders listed in records, questioning them. They'd be talking to some of the same ones. On the other cases, they'd found a few of those men alibied, and needn't cover those this time. They didn't know much about this X, but they did know he'd been the X on these other cases, because of Maggie Walters.

"Well, I'm blessed if I can give you any answer," said Dr. Goulding. Beside him, paunchy little Dr. Norenberg sighed; they both stared down at the opened corpse on the mortuary table. The family, Norenberg said, hadn't liked the idea of an autopsy, and it had been the better part of discretion not to move the corpse around; they'd borrowed a back room at the funeral parlor. And Goulding had been annoyed to be taken away from his own immediate autopsies, but like any good technician had got interested in the subject. He gently probed the exposed heart with one blunt finger. "Quite sound. How old did you say she was?"

"Seventy-nine," said Norenberg mournfully. "I'd been the family physician for twenty years. I can't make it out. Aside from the arthritis, she was in quite good condition. You can see she wasn't overweight, her blood pressure was very consistent, no diabetes, nothing. She was having a good deal of pain, of course, but she tolerated Darvon quite well, and she was getting excellent care, that's a good convalescent home."

"Not all of them are," said Goulding absently.

"I saw her the day before—last Thursday. My regular day there—I've got six patients there. She was a little depressed, but her blood pressure was excellent, she was having good regular elimination, appetite good—and then she popped off like that in her sleep, apparently. The nurse found her dead in bed on Friday morning. It bothered me," said Norenberg. "I suppose I should have let it go, what's the odds? She'd had a good life, what did it matter—but I felt I'd like to know."

"And we don't. Just as well if you had let it go," said Goulding. "But we might as well be thorough. You said she was depressed. Enough for suicide? Could she have got hold of something, an overdose of Darvon maybe?"

"Quite impossible, I'd say. But—"

"Explore every avenue as they say," said Goulding dryly. "We'll try to find out." Stomach contents, secretions, blood samples for the lab to look at.

"Damn it, what do I put on the certificate?" asked Norenberg. "It'll be a while before we get an analysis."

"Syncope. It covers a lot of things," said Goulding. He was a little curious about this one himself, but he had a more important job waiting back at the morgue. Having had a look at one of the bodies last night, he was fairly sure of what he'd find in the others. It wasn't pretty, and it was going to make a lot of work for the detectives; he could hear O'Connor swear now.

O'Connor had listened to Katz's little tale with interest, and agreed he'd better pass it on to Hollywood. Nothing immediately for them: it was business for the juvenile court.

Wayne had gone out to cover the inquest: just more paperwork. They wouldn't be hearing the results of those autopsies until later today, and meanwhile there was some work to do on this pair of heist-women. Burt was busy over those lifted prints. O'Connor started down to records to see if there were any female heisters on file, and was halted at the foot of the stairs by Sergeant Duff.

"Just going to send this up—I suppose you'll be putting out an A.P.B." He handed O'Connor a Telex sheet.

They had lifted some prints on the liquor-store job last week —that heister had dropped a paper bag with part of the loot when the store owner fired at him, and these days the lab could lift prints from nearly any surface. They hadn't been in Glendale's files, or those of any force around, so they'd been sent back to the FBI for a possible make; this was the kickback. The FBI had made him: one Clarence Gantman, pedigree of armed robbery, burglary, assault; he'd served time in the Illinois pen, in Iowa, and was six months out of a federal prison in Indiana. Caucasian, five-ten, a hundred and forty, forty-seven, brown and blue— "Get out the A.P.B.," said O'Connor, "and hope it turns him up." He stuck the Telex in his pocket and turned to go down to the records office, and then swung around at the woman's tired voice behind him.

"Please—could you tell me where we should go—it's about the accident last night. The traffic accident. I'm Mrs. Massey— this is my son Donald, and he—we want to—"

Duff caught O'Connor's eye. "Yes, ma'am. What accident would you mean?"

"The hit and run," said the thin boy beside her. He had a soft voice.

"Oh, sure. Maybe you'd like to talk to Lieutenant O'Connor here."

O'Connor went up to the desk. "A hit-run—should I know about it?"

"If you looked at the reports on your desk." Traffic reports wouldn't get up to the detective office unless they added up to a felony, which a hit-run did.

"O.K., O.K. I was concentrating on our female gunmen. Mrs. Massey? Would you like to come up to the office, please?" They followed him upstairs in silence. Katz was on the phone, the big fluorescent-lighted room otherwise empty. O'Connor offered them chairs and scrabbled through the papers on his desk. The hit-run had happened at seven-twenty at Central and Wilson; just by fool chance Gordon in a squad car had been cruising down Central and saw it, and took off after the car, calling in for backup. He hadn't got the plate number at night and during high-speed pursuit, but the car was an old white Dodge sedan, beat up: no make on the driver. Gordon had eventually lost it on the Golden State freeway, in medium-heavy traffic. The victim was Clarice Duffy, seventy-four, taken to the emergency hospital.

"So—about this hit-run," said O'Connor, and swiveled his chair round to face them. They looked at him dumbly. The woman was in her forties, once very pretty and still nice-looking, well dressed, discreet make-up. She'd been crying, and she was frightened; he saw the fear deepen in her eyes as she looked at him, and he sighed to himself. Sometimes the citizens wore that look, confronted by O'Connor the first time, the tough cop with the obvious bulge at the left shoulder where his favorite .357 magnum was a fixture most of his waking hours, with his heavy bulldog jaw and abrupt manner; and there wasn't any way to explain to them that he really didn't go round beating people up just for the fun of it. "You've got some information for us, Mrs. Massey?"

She nodded submissively. "This is my son Donald. He—I knew we had to come and tell you. It was only—"

The boy raised his head and looked at O'Connor, and he was frightened too. He wasn't the usual long-haired lout; he looked like a nice kid, about eighteen: medium-sized, dark blond hair neat and short, gray slacks and a blue sports shirt—a clean-cut boy. He said in his thin soft voice, "It was me. I just got scared. It was—so awful sudden. I'm a good driver, I never had a ticket, or an accident of any kind. I know I should've stopped—I was just scared."

"All right," said O'Connor easily, leaning back. "Tell me how it happened."

The boy relaxed a little and took a long breath. "I—was on my way home, see. We live up on Mountain. I'd been to a movie with Tim and Bill, and took them home, and I was heading home. I was making a right onto Central. I waited for the sign, sir, honest. Till it stopped flashing WALK and said WAIT—there were people crossing Central and I waited till they were all past, see. And then I turned, I never saw that lady till I—till I hit her, it was dark and she had on dark clothes and—it was just, all of a sudden there she *was*, and I hit the brake but there wasn't time, I knew I hit her, and then I heard the siren behind me and —I got scared and just sort of took off. I know it was wrong—I'm sorry."

"I just got it out of him this morning," said Mrs. Massey shakily. "I knew there was something wrong—and I knew we had to come and tell—"

"That's right," said O'Connor. "We're glad you did."

"Will there—be a fine, or my license suspended, or what? I'm awful sorry, I just never thought a thing like that could happen to me—but—"

"Well, let's do a little checking," said O'Connor. He took up the phone and told Duff to get him the hospital. The Masseys just sat in fearful silence. He got the emergency floor and was handed around a little, finally talked to a no-nonsense-sounding nurse.

"Oh, that one. The accident. Brought in about eight last night? She died about midnight, I've just been trying to contact her daughter in San Francisco. What? Oh, it was massive internal hemmorhage—the car went right over her, there was never a chance she'd live."

"Thanks so much," said O'Connor. As a rule he liked his job, though he groused about it now and then; and he didn't mind what happened to the thugs and hoods who preyed on the citizenry and just occasionally got their comeuppance. But he hated the things like this, when the innocent citizen was involved. Easy to say, his own fault: he shouldn't have panicked. There was nothing very new about human nature.

"Mrs. Massey, would you like to call your husband?" he asked abruptly.

"He's dead," she said faintly. "Three years ago. Why? What did you find out just now?"

O'Connor sighed and started to tell them. It would be a manslaughter charge, and if the boy had stopped probably dismissed as involuntary; now, he could end up with a one-to-three. It was a sad and sorry thing, but that cops saw a good deal of.

Before going back to the office to look at the files of sex offenders, Varallo and Forbes, being thorough, had knocked on doors on either side of the apartment house, hoping that some other latecomer had noticed X. They drew blank on it, but it used up time; they picked up an early lunch and got back to the station at twelve-ten to find O'Connor swearing at the typewriter and Katz still on the phone.

"How I hate these damned things," said O'Connor, and gave them a brief rundown on the hit-run. "Basically a good kid, and just a minute's panic—oh, hell take the goddamned machine!" Irritably he disentangled jammed keys. "You turn up anything?"

"Something," said Varallo. "Nothing new gone down? So now we start to do the legwork all over again. Sex offenders out of the files. And a heat wave getting under way." And, which he didn't add, all his roses needing spraying and feeding. He hadn't got that Pedrálbes to bloom yet, and last night when he'd finally got home there'd been aphids all over Alida Lovett. Maybe a funny kind of hobby for a cop, but—.

"I do not," said Katz, "think any of these head doctors have any sense at all."

"Amen," said Forbes. "Did you just decide that?"

"I've been talking to the one this Finch girl's going to. By order of the court. I think he's nuts too," said Katz. He loosened his tie and sat back in his chair. "The girl's a very interesting case, he says to me—I spare you the double-talk. Classic case of suppressed hostility. One sees it has been difficult for the parents, he says—the girl's clinically impervious to pain, it's been no use to punish her. D'you know they once caught her cutting up a cat with a butcher knife to find its purr? He says to me, very interesting, complete apparent lack of all empathy. Those kids she was baby-sitting—they got to yelling, and annoyed her, so she tied 'em up with clothesline and locked them in a closet. Just luck they didn't suffocate. Brother."

"*Dio*," said Varallo.

"And then he says to me, he doesn't recommend restraint for her at this time, it would only aggravate her hostilities. If you ask me," said Katz, "speaking just as a layman of, I hope, some common sense, that girl's just as apt to try poisoning a person as a dog, and she probably will if she isn't locked up. But at least for the moment it's not our baby. I think I'll go have lunch." He yawned and stood up.

"And we had better get to the legwork, Jeff." Reluctantly Varallo unfolded himself from the chair. "Weed out some of those files downstairs. We might turn lucky this time, with a vague description."

As they rounded the bend in the staircase they could hear a donnybrook of some sort going on below: Duff's voice raised, and another man shouting. "Now what the hell?" said Forbes.

In the lobby two uniformed men, Fenner and Judovic, were trying to talk to a civilian, and Duff had come out from behind the desk and was repeating, "Now, Mr. Pinney, if you'd just calm down—now, Mr. Pinney—" None of them was getting anywhere. At first glance the civilian appeared to be on the verge of a stroke, but Varallo diagnosed his state with a second look. Mr. Pinney was sizzling mad and he didn't care who knew it. He was practically giving off sparks.

"The law is the law! The law is the law!" shouted Mr. Pinney, bouncing back and forth and waving his arms at the three uniforms. "Cops are not above the law any more than anybody else is! I may not have a goddamned college degree but that I do know—and by God, if your superior officers try to back you up and give me any back talk, I'll go to the mayor—I'll go to the city council—I'll go to the—"

"What's going on here?" asked Forbes loudly. They all turned to the detectives and Pinney pounced at Varallo like a cat.

"Are you officers? Police officers? Superior to these two men?" He was a round, bald man with a red face, burly shoulders and a surprising deep bass voice. He was wearing a rumpled navy suit and a shirt that had seen better days.

"Well, yes. Why? What's the trouble here?"

"Sir—it was a *call*," said Fenner. "Look, he raised such a fuss we brought him in for somebody to talk to—"

"The law is the law! That man deserves a ticket! I want to see him get a ticket!" Pinney was stuttering with fury. "I saw the whole thing, and anybody else would get the book thrown at him for double-parking! Do I know the rules and regulations? My God, do I know! Go to get my damn license renewed, I've never had a ticket in my life—safest driver on the road for thirty years —and they throw these damn loaded questions at me, what the hell do I know about what it's illegal to do to a muffler, and that goddamned, arrogant S.O.B. says I have to take the test again. Do *I* know the book? Do I?" He fumbled in his pocket and pro- duced a copy of the California Driver's Handbook and shook it menacingly under Fenner's nose.

"Listen," said Judovic, "it was a Code Three—red light and Siren. This bar down on South Central. We—"

"Now you listen to this," panted Pinney, leafing over pages. "Here it is in black and white. *Prohibited Parking. Do not stop, park, or leave your car in any of the following places, V.C. Sec. 22500. Within an intersection, on a crosswalk or sidewalk, on the roadway side of any car parked at the curb (double-parking).* And he did! He did! I was just getting into my car when he double-parked right up against me and left the car and went into that bar! And I was late for an appointment already and it was a goddamned nuisance, and he ought to get a ticket!"

Forbes started to laugh. "What was the call?" asked Varallo, restraining himself.

"Ah, nothing," said Judovic. "But we didn't know—it was a Code Three. This guy pulled a gun and the bartender thought it was a heist and called in, but it turned out he was just showing it to another guy wanted to buy it. But naturally we were in a hurry, Mike piled out of the squad after me—I'd got there first —and when we came out—ah—Mr. Pinney was having kittens. We tried to—"

"Mmh, yes," said Varallo. "Now please, just calm down,

sir—" But it took awhile to get it through Mr. Pinney's head that a law-enforcement officer on urgent business can leave his vehicle anywhere convenient without being subject to traffic tickets. Reluctantly he started to leave; balefully he announced his opinion that cops just stuck together and it was lot of god-damned double-talk.

Fenner and Judovic went back on tour. Varallo and Forbes went on down to records for a list of the possible X's on Stephanie.

O'Connor finished the report on the hit-run, and before going out for lunch consulted records about any females with armed robbery in their pedigrees. He didn't expect to find many: other forces around, especially LAPD, might have more, but there was just one in Glendale's records: Marcia Olson, address up on Palm Drive. The record dated back two years: attempted heist of a dairy store, first offense, suspended sentence and probation. Well, it was a place to start.

He stopped for a sandwich and tried the address on Palm. Nobody was home; an incurious neighbor out in the next yard told him that Marcia worked at the Deelicious Chicken Hut on Chevy Chase and her mother was visiting relatives back East.

The Deelicious Chicken Hut was one of those take-out places, a hole in the wall sandwiched between a gas station and a plumbing company. O'Connor went in and flashed the badge at the pert blond behind the little counter. "I'm looking for Marcia Olson."

"And what does a cop want with me?" she asked, ready to flare up. "Yes, that's me. What about it?"

"Just a few questions, Miss Olson. Where were you last night at about eight o'clock?"

"Right here," she came back smartly. "We're open till nine on Sundays. And four people back there can tell you so, too. Why in—well, just why d'you want to know, anyway?"

"You've got a little record," said O'Connor.

She looked astonished and then started to laugh. "What do

you—oh, my God, that old thing? That? A couple of years ago? I was still in high, just a fool kid, and Dave dared me—"

Even before he talked to the other four employees, O'Connor knew this was a waste of time. But he asked, and her alibi got backed up.

He went back to the office and asked Burt what he'd got out of the prints. "Nothing yet," said Burt. "Three of them belonged to the night clerk and the rest don't show in our records. I've sent them to LAPD and Pasadena and Washington. Wait for the kickbacks."

"You're a philosopher," said O'Connor. He wondered if Mrs. Massey had talked to a lawyer yet. There'd be red tape on it; the warrant hadn't come through yet and Donald was sitting over in the jail, but eventually there'd be bail. He sat at his desk wondering where to go on the heisters, if nobody knew the prints, and of course there wasn't anywhere. Ten minutes later Duff buzzed him from the desk.

"I just thought you'd like to know—Traffic's got a sniper on the Ventura freeway. Somewhere around San Fernando Road. So far, one man hit and a little pileup—they've shut down traffic east and west."

"I'm on my way!" O'Connor leaped up, feeling the shoulder holster. As he passed the desk downstairs Duff grinned at him.

"Just in case they need a top shooter to gun him down, Lieutenant?"

And O'Connor meant to hang onto that top-marksman medal from the California Peace Officers Association; he ought to get in more target practice these days.

The freeway was backed up with traffic and irate drivers using their horns. Senseless damned fools, he thought, leaning out to beckon a cycle officer; they might know there was some reason. He flashed the badge. "Have they got him spotted? Where? Can you get me up there?"

"Yessir—CHP's out on it too—we think he's somewhere up the hill from the overpass at San Fernando. I'll get you through —they're setting up a command post on Doran—"

It was a little anticlimax, after a ride behind the siren, to find that the sniper was already in custody. He'd been plugged in one arm by a CHP man but wasn't much hurt. He was a weedy, spectacled young fellow with a pimply pale face and whitely rolling eyes; they'd taken a new British Enfield rifle away from him.

"But I was just getting the trajectory right," he kept saying to the CHP man. "I been studying trajectories—I was just getting it, but all the cars stopped coming—"

"Yeah, we're always spoiling people's fun," said the CHP man. "Now I've got to tell you all about your rights—"

There were eighteen possibles for the rapist out of records, who conformed more or less to the vague description. Varallo and Forbes split them up and went out on the legwork, in the heat wave; it had got up to ninety-three today.

Three of the ones Varallo was hunting had moved away; they were all off probation, so there was nothing illegal about that. The next one had voluntarily committed himself to Camarillo. The fifth one, Richard Moore, one count of rape and still on parole, was at home; Varallo brought him in to question, and got nothing at all. He didn't have an alibi for Saturday night or early Sunday morning; he lived alone in a cheap room in a hotel on Jackson Street. He said he hadn't done nothing, nothing at all, and maybe he hadn't. In a general way he matched what description they had: five-eight, thin, twenty-seven. He could be, he might not be; it was all up in the air. It would be no use to arrange a lineup, let Stephanie and the other two girls look at him; they couldn't say for sure, for any legal charge. Varallo let him go and went out hunting again.

He found another one like that: Jay Kleinman, two counts of rape, indecent exposure, narco, still on parole from Folsom. He lived alone in an apartment in Montrose, and he said he was clean, he hadn't been doing nothing, but there was no alibi to back him up. "What the hell, cop, you damn guys want it both ways? I ain't married, and on P.A. yet I ain't s'posed to have no chicks or see guys I know got pedigrees too—what the hell you expect, anyways?" Annoyingly, of course that made some sense; but it left him up in the air too. Quite often the legwork was a waste of time, but you had to start somewhere.

At five forty-five Varallo was up in La Crescenta, listening to a solid alibi from Albert Weaver, one count of attempted rape, one statutory rape. He'd been at a party to celebrate his grand-parents' golden wedding anniversary on Saturday night and early Sunday morning, and all the members of a large family could say so. He offered names and addresses eagerly.

Getting into the Gremlin, Varallo decided to call it a day; and a fairly unproductive day it had been. Of course, they should hear something about those bodies presently, and that would make more work. And what that might turn out to be—

He turned into the drive of the house on Hillcroft Road at six-thirty. Going in the back door, he cast a bitter look at Alida Lovett climbing up the patio trellis. Those goddamned aphids—and he wasn't off until Wednesday. "Good day, darling?" asked Laura as he kissed her. "You've got time for a drink if you want one."

"Maybe I need one." But first he wandered down the hall to see their best baby, darling Ginevra; she was happily engaged in her playpen with the big stuffed gray cat Katharine had given her for her first birthday in January, and she lifted her arms to Varallo with a wide, dimpled smile.

"Day-dee! Pat Gidden!" she demanded. She was, of course, a remarkably intelligent child, already talking so well. The proto-type of the stuffed cat, the gray tiger Gideon Algernon Cad-wallader, was playing watch-cat on the dresser; he blinked green eyes at Varallo.

At five-fifteen the CHP called in and O'Connor talked to a Captain Dennis. "We thought you'd be interested to know about your sniper. We checked him out through the car registra-tion—maybe you did too."

"We're a little shorthanded here," said O'Connor. "I haven't heard—Traffic was on it."

"Yeah. Well, he's been in and out of Camarillo, tagged a schizo. No driver's license, so that'll be another charge—he'd borrowed his mother's car. Silly damn female—she just said everybody always picks on poor Bobby. His name's Bobby Holt."

"Yeah," said O'Connor. "What about the gun?"

"He won't say where he got that, at least he hadn't up to the time your boys took him in. He'll probably end up back in Camarillo."

"Until they let him out again," said O'Connor. "At least nobody got killed."

And these days, of course, the computers made shortcuts sometimes. They got a kickback from LAPD ten minutes later; the prints from the pharmacy register were unknown to them. "Wait to see what Washington says," said Burt, relaying that to O'Connor. "But I tell you, I've got the hunch this is a pair of amateurs. They won't be in anybody's records. And on the other hand, we don't know for sure that any of these damned prints belong to them. Sometimes I feel as if *we're* amateurs, the way we have to go at things."

Everybody else had gone, and Bob Rhys had just come in a little early, when O'Connor started downstairs at five past six. They'd just had a kickback from Pasadena; they didn't know the prints either. Probably Burt was right.

Goulding was just coming up the hall into the lobby. "I hoped I'd catch you. The sooner you get on this one the better."

"So what can you tell us?" They sat down on the vinyl couch just inside the front door. "You've had a look inside—what showed?"

Goulding sighed, getting out a cigar. The big building was very quiet; Traffic shift had changed two hours ago. Sergeant Ray Harrison had just taken over the desk, and now Dick Hunter came in hurriedly, ten minutes late—O'Connor frowned at him—and went up the stairs without speaking.

"You may have a little lead." Goulding sounded tired. "But it's the hell of a thing, Charles. You want facts, not guesses. The two older kids are boys. Somewhere around four and two. There was malnutrition—neither of them had been getting much to eat for a while—but the actual cause of death was the same for both of them. Their throats had been cut with a fairly blunt knife."

"Jesus," said O'Connor. "Two and four. And?"

"The baby. A girl, under six months I'd say. They were all undersized, probably they'd never been fed decently. There was a skull fracture in the baby, but she actually died of suffocation. If you want an educated guess, considering how we found them, could be they were dumped up there together and whoever did it thought the baby was dead, she landed under the other two bodies and *kaput*."

"Christ. When?"

"Just a guess—a lot of factors enter in, weather, terrain, temperature—between one and two months."

"You said maybe a lead. What?"

"A funny thing," said Goulding. "I just passed it up to the lab, caught Burt before he left—he was interested. The clothes— you won't get much there. There was only one label left—Sears, mass-produced stuff. But there was a bracelet on the baby's arm —minor miracle it was still partly intact. What it looks like is the standard plastic name-tag they put on at the hospital at birth. No, don't ask—you never get it that easy—it's not legible, it's ready to fall apart, but infrared might bring out something."

"For God's sake!" said O'Connor. "You said, the baby maybe five or six months old? That thing left on?"

"Sometimes I get tired, Charles. The things we see. Those kids were neglected from the start. People—"

"Oh yes," said O'Connor. "Oh yes, Doctor. People. Thanks so much—we'll see what the lab can turn up." He felt a little tired himself.

When he turned into the drive of the house on Virginia Avenue, and got out to open the gate, Maisie told the world that Master was home and pounced at him delightedly. "Get down!" said O'Connor, staggering against the gate.

In the kitchen, Katharine was busy at the stove. "If you want a drink before dinner, I'll have one too. Of course it's all right, idiot, I asked the doctor. Have you found out anything else about those poor children?"

"Now, Katy—talking about horrors isn't so good for you maybe—"

"Men!" said Katharine impatiently. "I never felt better in my life."

# THREE

The first piece of business for the night watch was a Telex from Sacramento. When the Feds had identified Clarence Gantman as last week's heister, an automatic query had gone up to the D.M.V. about a possible car. Now they got a make on a 1971 Ford two-door, plate number thus and such, registered to an address on Elmwood in Burbank. Rhys added that to the A.P.B. already out, and just on the chance he and Hunter went over to Burbank to look.

It was a ramshackle little frame house, and the door was jerked open ten seconds after Rhys shoved the bell. The man who opened it wasn't Gantman, ten years older and forty pounds heavier. "Who are you? What the hell, cops?" He stared at the badges. "You want him for something?"

"Who?" asked Rhys. "We're looking for a Clarence Gantman."

"Yeah, yeah, that's the name he said. Whatever you want him for, you can add on he owes me four hundred in rent. Two months he owed me—I been after him, he finally gives me a check yesterday, and today it bounces, so I come to throw him out and he's skipped. Him and that girl, I guess she was living with him. Left a mess—refrigerator half full of spoiled stuff —renters, my God! What do you want him for?"

They looked around, but there wasn't anything to say where Gantman might have gone, and the owner didn't even know the girl's name. They offered him sympathy and went back to Glendale.

At eight-forty they got a call from Traffic: a heist at a liquor store, the Red Carpet out on East Glenoaks. When they got there one black-and-white was just pulling out from the curb; Stoner was still talking to two men at the counter. One of them turned out to be the manager, Ed Nelson.

"Describe him?" he said to the detectives indignantly. "I can sure as hell describe him, and so can Fred—these damn punks are getting too big for their britches lately—walk in here and show the gun, not even a hat on, does he think we're blind or just as stupid as he is, for God's sake? He was about twenty-six, twenty-seven, five-ten, not fat or thin, brown hair, I'd spot him anywhere—he had a kind of three-cornered scar on his chin—"

"Any idea what the gun was?" asked Rhys.

"A big one—revolver. At least he didn't get much," said Nelson. "We were just about to close, I'd already cleaned the register out, just left enough change to start in the morning, and the bank deposit bag was in my car. But these damn punks—"

Time was, Rhys said to Hunter on the way back to the station, weeks would go by in Glendale without a heist. Maybe Hunter, who was only five years on the force and a newly ranking plainclothes man, didn't quite believe him. Well, Hunter could write up the report.

When they walked in the front door, two Traffic men were waiting for them with a little more business. One drunk civilian and one sober, the sober one sporting the start of a black eye and a cut lip. Gordon filled Rhys in while Hunter went on up to start the report.

"It was just a simple 502, looked like. The drunk ran into this Reinhart over on Broadway, and Reinhart was mad as hell, he was driving a brand-new Caddy and the front end's a mess. They were going at each other hammer and tongs when Bill and I got there, and the drunk got in a couple of lucky punches, which just made Reinhart all the madder. He's going to sue him but he wants to see him charged with assault first. We couldn't find any I.D. on the drunk."

Rhys surveyed the pair with exasperation; tempest in a teapot. Reinhart looked like an upright citizen, a man about fifty, well-dressed; he had calmed down, was leaning on the desk dabbing at his lip with a handkerchief. The drunk had gone peacefully to sleep in a chair, a paunchy, elderly man in shabby sports clothes. Just more paperwork, thought Rhys, annoyed.

"You'd better take him over to the tank—we'll talk to him tomorrow and find out who he is. Mr. Reinhart? If you'd come up to the office, I'll take a statement from you about this. Are you feeling all right, sir?" Reinhart looked pale and was breathing rather quickly.

"Yes, sure. You're damn right I want to make a statement— and what do you want to bet that bum hasn't got any insurance? I'd better call my wife and tell her why I'm late, if that's all right."

"Yes, sir." The uniformed men were hauling the drunk out. Reinhart puffed a little, climbing the stairs behind Rhys, and Rhys pulled out a chair for him. Hunter was hunched over his typewriter across the room. "You can use this phone, sir."

"Thanks," said Reinhart, and with no warning added a faint cough and slid to the floor to sprawl full length.

"Damn," said Rhys. Gordon said the man had taken a punch or two. Delayed concussion, could be. Rhys bent over him, and after a minute realized there wasn't any pulse at all. "Dick!" he called urgently, and started artificial respiration. Five minutes later there was still no response and Hunter put in a call to the paramedics. They got there in another five minutes and brought out all their paraphernalia, but they couldn't bring him back.

"For God's sake," said Rhys, shaken, "but what was it? He'd been in a little fight—concussion maybe—but he seemed O.K., unless it was his heart all of a sudden—"

"The autopsy'll tell you," said one of the paramedics cynically, packing equipment away. "It was cardiac arrest but that could be a hundred things."

Rhys and Hunter were still shaken. They took Reinhart's wallet for the address: another job cops came in for that had to be done, informing next of kin. But there was only his wife listed as whom to notify, and Rhys didn't think it was such a good idea to call her on the phone at eleven o'clock to tell her she was a widow. The address was on Kenneth Road; he drove up there, and of course it was a little mess. She was alone in the house, and she went to pieces after asking him to call her son-in-law; he had to call an ambulance too, and waited to tell the son-in-law about it. Then he went back to the station to write a report. The body had been taken over to the morgue.

If the autopsy showed the drunk's punch had anything to do with it, there'd be a manslaughter charge, and more paperwork on that.

When O'Connor got in on Tuesday morning, he only grunted over the report on Reinhart; but glancing at Hunter's report on the heist, he said disgustedly, "Now that is the goddamndest stupid thing! These silly little louts—I swear to God, Vic, I get tired." He shoved the report across his desk. "Bob should have spotted that—or maybe I've pulled this one in oftener, come to think. My God." He sat back and lit a cigarette, set the lighter down with a bang.

"Spotted what? It was a fairly stupid effort, I see—"

"Fairly? With his bare face hanging out he pulls a heist eight blocks from where he lives, and he's got to be on P.A. —I didn't know he was out. You ought to remember him—we picked him up for the same thing six months ago. Robert Eldridge, pedigree back to age twelve. He got that scar on his chin in a knife fight when he was in Vacaville the first time."

"Oh—that one. I'd forgotten his name. He pulled a one-to-three in March," said Varallo.

"And he's out—par for the course," said O'Connor grimly. "These goddamned softheaded judges—and no bets he'll stay in much longer this time. But we'd better go see if we can pick him up. You might look up the address in records—it's somewhere on Ethel, I think. I'll meet you downstairs."

Still muttering about that, he went across the hall to the little lab. "Goulding told me about that thing—are you getting anywhere with it?"

"Early to say," said Thomsen. "It's a tricky little job. That's the damndest thing we've had in a while, these kids. And this is pretty far gone. Rex thinks we can use oblique light to bring it out, but it'll be a job. Want to see it?" He led O'Connor into the little darkroom where Burt was bent over the bench.

They had it centered on a square of dark cloth as contrast, with a strong overhead light. It was just a scrap of thing, not a quarter of an inch wide, stained and dirty plastic with a minute area at one end discolored darker. O'Connor stared at it. "You'll never get anything out of that." He wouldn't have guessed what it was himself; and Goulding could be wrong about that, too.

"Have a try at it," said Burt. "Surprising what shows up under infrared."

"Could you get any prints from the bodies?" asked O'Connor.

"N.G.," said Thomsen. "Too far gone. If this doesn't show us something, we can try injecting the fingers, pump them up far enough for prints—but would kids that young be on file anywhere? I can tell you now, it'd be impossible to get a footprint from the baby."

"Helpful," said O'Connor. And it would also be impossible to run pictures of the kids' faces, to see if anybody recognized them. They might never get them identified; right now he doubted they would. Three kids, starved and killed and dumped up there— As a good cop, he wasn't given to getting emotional about the cases that came along to be worked, but sometimes it was hard not to. He went downstairs to find Varallo waiting.

"Take your car in case we pick him up. What are you annoyed about now?"

O'Connor told him as they went out to the lot. "And if he is there, pick him up and go through the motions, shove him back in and he'll be out in another three months. He lives with his mother—silly dreep of a woman, gives him an allowance for sitting around calling her Mama."

"So why is he knocking over cash registers?"

"Because he's built that way, damn it," said O'Connor.

It was a comfortable old house, well enough kept up, in that older residential area. The woman who opened the door to them stared at O'Connor and put one hand to her mouth. She was gray-haired and fat, with foolish eyes and a rabbity chin.

"Oh, dear—has he—has he done something else?" she quavered.

"Is he here?" asked O'Connor. She nodded and stepped back. O'Connor marched in and paused on the top step of a sunken living room. "You stupid little punk," he said, "come to Papa. You're going back to the joint."

Eldridge, hunched over a western magazine, looked up slowly. The liquor-store manager had described his salient points, but hadn't mentioned the dull little eyes, the generally vacuous expression. He looked aggrieved and surprised. "I haven't done nothing," he said.

"Oh, my God," said O'Connor. "When two men can pick you out of a lineup half a mile away. Come on, Dicky. Don't waste our time."

They found the gun in plain sight on a stack of magazines in the living room, an old Colt .38. Eldridge wouldn't say where he'd got it, but in the last thirteen years he'd made a lot of pals on the wrong side of the law.

They took him back to the station and booked him in, and Varallo spent a little while arranging a lineup for that afternoon, contacting the store manager and clerk. It was the kind of tedious routine that had to be done, using up time. And he'd take no bets that O'Connor wasn't right, Eldridge out again in a few months. It was frustrating to any cop, and nothing they could do about it.

Katz and Forbes had gone out looking for sex offenders. "It just occurs to me," said Katz, "that it wouldn't do any harm to ask NCIC again, Jeff. I know we did before, on the Maggie Walters angle, but when you come to think, where's he been? He pulls two rapes fairly close together last January, and then nothing—now six months later here he is again. What sets him off? Not the full moon or we'd have heard from him sooner."

"So, could be he's been somewhere else. It won't do any harm to find out," agreed Forbes. They sent an inquiry to NCIC, that useful clearing house of crime, and split up the remaining names from the list.

The first one Katz found was Rudolph Schroeder, one count of rape and now off P.A.; he'd just been laid off a job at Lockheed and was recovering from a hangover at home, which was a sleazy apartment in Montrose. He answered Katz blearily, resigned to cops coming around. "When 'd you say? Last Saturday—Sunday morning—oh-oh, you can't pin anything on me for then, not no way. I was in a little poker session over at Eddy's—seven-eight of the guys, we started in maybe eight Saturday night and it lasted all night up to when Eddy's wife broke it up about noon on Sunday. What? Oh, sure, you go and ask any of 'em—but especially you ask Eddy's wife, see, she was sure sore about it—she prob'ly wouldn't' a' been if he'd won anything, but he dropped two weeks' pay and that woman was fit to be tied, I tell you."

He provided names and addresses, and Katz checked out a couple of them; the alibi stood up, and while they were rough-and-ready types, none of them had any pedigrees; it was all kosher. He got back to the station at eleven-forty to find Forbes just in with a slightly hotter suspect who didn't have an alibi, and they took him into an interrogation room and started to ask questions. But it was all very unsatisfactory, up in the air; he could be, he couldn't be.

"And," said Katz ruminatively after they'd let him go, "he didn't show any reaction to Maggie Walters. I think our boy would—he's got some kind of hangup on that, and if he's not legally nuts he's not a hundred per cent normal. I don't think we'll drop on him this way."

But there were still a few more to find and look at. Varallo was just back from setting up that lineup; they stopped for an early lunch at the new little place around the corner and went on with the legwork.

Varallo came back at two-thirty, having drawn a blank on all four men he'd been hunting; two had moved and two had alibis. Forbes and Katz were still out, and O'Connor was under siege at his desk with a fat young woman sobbing violently on one side of him and a fat middle-aged woman shouting at him from the other.

"And why the hell you can't keep him in jail once you got him—you let the big basser out an' the next thing he's drunk again and beatin' up the kids—takin' all the welfare money! Some day he's gonna kill her or one of the kids, I swear to God, and if you'd just keep the big basser in jail—"

"Mrs. Tillman, it isn't up to the police—if you'd just calm down now, please—" O'Connor looked harassed. "A common drunk charge isn't—"

"Half killed her already, just look at her! I told her she'd be sorry she married the big basser, but girls don't never listen to their mothers—"

The young woman burst out in fresh wails, and O'Connor raised his voice. "If Mrs. Thomas wants to sign a complaint against him, charge him with assault, we can arrest him, but—"

"That's what I told her, just like that thing says, change the name an' not the letter, change for worse— What'd you say? Sign a—you better just bet she'll sign a complaint! I'll see she signs it all right! Lorna, for God's sake stop that blubbering and listen to this cop—"

Varallo exchanged a glance with O'Connor and went on to his desk; the phone light was flashing and he picked up the phone. "I just had a call from Wilcox Street," said Duff. "They've spotted that Gantman's car."

"I didn't know we'd tied him to one."

"Yeah, the D.M.V. came through last night and it got added to the A.P.B. Squad car just spotted it parked over in the Atwater district and called it in. Addison Drive. They said they'd stand by till somebody got there."

"Right," said Varallo, "I'm on it." He started downstairs again and met Katz coming up, and turned him around by one arm. "He's wanted for armed robbery after all, Joe—you may as

well come along. Gantman. LAPD just made his car over in
Atwater. We'd better take your car."

"In case we pick him up. If you ask me," said Katz, fishing
out his keys, "half the reason you got yourself that—that kiddie-
car is so you can't go collecting people in it. Barely room for
you. I suppose you save enough on gas that you don't care
about putting in for mileage."

"Oh, she's a nice little girl, Joe. Very handy," grinned Varallo.
"Better step on it, LAPD's standing by over there."

The block they wanted on Addison Drive was a tired old
block of shabby four- and six-family apartment houses. They
spotted the black-and-white a block up, parked around the
corner, and Katz slowed and swung around beside it. The uniformed man leaned out. "You the boys from Glendale? I
thought I'd better not spook him by advertising the presence, if
he's anywhere around. The block dead-ends down there, he'd
have to come out this way, but the car's still there. Good luck
on it."

"Thanks very much, we'll have a look . . . And if he isn't
anywhere around," said Katz, swinging the wheel, "we'll have
to stake it out. But then, come to think, he had to find somewhere else to live. With or without girl friend. Didn't you see
Bob's report? There was an address from the D.M.V., naturally
they checked it—Gantman'd run out on his landlord."

"So we have a look around." The Ford registered to Gantman
was parked at the curb in front of a four-family apartment. The
place had started life as a single two-story house, been cut up in
a makeshift way: there were only two front doors, and only one
bore a name plate: Robertson. The other door was open, and just
inside was a flight of stairs going up from a tiny box of a lobby,
and another door at right angles. Varallo knocked on that.

An elderly man opened it promptly and blinked at them.
"Yes?"

"We're looking for a Mr. Gantman. Do you know if he
lives here, sir?"

"There's a new tenant upstairs—I don't know his name. He

just moved in yesterday, seems to be a nice fellow. What? Oh, it's the right side, straight up. Could be your friend, I didn't catch his name like I said—you're welcome, I'm sure."

"New roof over his head, I told you," said Katz. They climbed rickety stairs and he knocked at the door on the right at the top, two doors three feet apart on a tiny landing. They waited. The door was jerked open violently.

"I told you I'd hand over the extra month soon as I got p—— Who the hell are you?" It was Gantman all right. They both had their badges out. "Oh, for Christ's sake!" said Gantman, and exploded between them, making a desperate try for the stairs. It wasn't a very handy spot for any kind of fight. Varallo grabbed for him and got one arm, pulled him around, and Gantman aimed a wild blow that connected with Varallo's shoulder and staggered him back. Gantman turned to plunge for the stairs and Katz collared him from behind, but he wasn't as big as Gantman, and with a roar Gantman shook him partly loose, lunged forward, tripped on a loose stair tread and sailed sprawling down the full flight, yanking Katz along with him.

Varallo leaped after them. "Joe—you O.K.?" Katz had landed half under the bigger man; he crawled over to sit on the bottom step.

"I dod't kdow." He clutched his nose.

Gantman had knocked himself out; Varallo got out the cuffs and slapped them on before he could come to and make any more trouble.

Katz fumbled out his handkerchief; his nose was bleeding copiously. "Dab it," he said querulously, "I'll bet it's broked—all I deed is adother bulge id my dose! The bastard! Does it look broked?" He emerged from the handkerchief.

"You'd better ask a doctor. You O.K. to drive?"

"Do," said Katz bitterly. "I'b bleeding like a stuck pig. Dab this bastard. Is he dead, I hope?"

"Not quite." Varallo slapped Gantman's face a few times, and he groaned and stirred, sat up, and swore at the hand-cuffs. Varallo hauled him up and got him out to the car, and

Katz handed him the keys. He went on bleeding all the way back to Glendale, and Varallo shepherded him into First Aid before he booked Gantman in. At least it was almost end of shift, and tomorrow was his day off.

When he got up to the office, O'Connor was wearing his sharklike grin. He'd just come back from the lineup, and Eldridge had been positively identified by Nelson and the clerk. Something tied up, anyway.

"I hope," said Rhys, "we don't have any more excitement tonight, Dick. My God, that was a damn queer thing to see. I wonder if they've found out what killed him."

"Probably his own fault," said Hunter from the wisdom of twenty-seven years. "An old guy like that going fighting, and he was too fat—out of condition."

"Well, it depends where you sit," said Rhys from seven years' more experience. "I'd just as soon have a quiet night. I hope Mother doesn't have to call the vet, Candy's been in labor a couple of hours."

"The vet? Oh, your mother's dog."

"This could be a champion litter." Rhys's mother bred Cairn terriers. "Oh-oh, a call this early. Don't tell me it's going to be that kind of night. Rhys."

"You've got a heist," said Harrison. "A market on Los Feliz."

"Hell and damnation," said Rhys. "All right, we're on it."

When they got there Gordon was waiting for them, another uniformed man inside. "It was this pair of females again," said Gordon. "The heisters. I heard something about it from Tracy —the damndest thing. Two women with a baby. They didn't get much this time."

"Well, I will be damned," said Rhys. "Going at it hot and heavy, aren't they? The first one got pulled Sunday, I think."

They had seen the reports on that, and now they heard the same descriptions, from this checker. One brown-haired, middle height, one blond, taller. The baby. And apparently there had been some rudimentary planning on the job. Between six and seven-thirty, the dinner hour, business was slow; there hadn't been any other customers in. The manager was in his office, two checkers on coffee breaks, only one stand open. "Honestly, I was just so surprised!" said the checker. "I was so surprised! They looked so ordinary—and a baby! I didn't have time to be scared— I was just so surprised! They looked so ordinary—honestly!" She couldn't say for certain how much they'd got, but less than a hundred dollars; she hadn't had much change left after a busy afternoon.

"Honestly is right," grumbled Rhys. "No leads at all, and no way to look for them. The lieutenant'll be annoyed." Just another report to type.

He was in the middle of that when his mother called. There were four nice pups, two of each, and mother and children fine.

O'Connor came in late on Wednesday morning, and swore over Rhys's report. "This damned pair," he said, shoving it over to Wayne. "The amateurs, and no way to go looking—damn all. Naturally the Feds don't know those prints, and it's ten to one they aren't the heisters' prints anyway. We can't even pinpoint one area—look at the places they've hit, for God's sake— market on Glenoaks, the professional building on Central, market on Los Feliz—miles apart. Of course they've got a car, but nobody's seen them in it, it's all up in the air."

"Offbeat," agreed Wayne lazily. And cops complained about the routine, but in dealing with routine crime it generally took them somewhere; on the odd ones, no. "I hope Joe's all right, he hasn't showed—I understand he was in a little ruckus yesterday."

O'Connor, muttering to himself, went over to the lab. "Have you got anywhere on that thing?" He laid a hand on the darkroom door and Thomsen yelped at him.

"Leave that alone, Rex always forgets to lock it. He's working on it now. Give us time—you can't rush these things. We'll let you know."

O'Connor went back to the detective office and met Wayne

and Forbes just going out. "Break-in just went down," said Wayne. "Furniture store on Colorado, the owner just came in to open up and found it."

"Always something," said O'Connor sourly. "Have fun." Poor was on the phone, sounding patient.

"Well, but what's it about?—doesn't sound like much, I mean there's no evidence of—what? Oh. Well, it still doesn't sound like much, Tracy. All right, all right, we have to come running when the citizen yells for cops. What school? . . . Oh. The ambulance—oh, I see. All right, I'll come out and talk to her."

"What's that all about?" O'Connor flung himself into his chair and it creaked protestingly.

"Probably nothing. School nurse wants cops—I'll check it out."

O'Connor sat at the desk and smoked several cigarettes too fast. He didn't think Burt was going to turn up any lead from that useless scrap of whatever it was. There wasn't going to be any easy way to identify those bodies—maybe no way. All right, they couldn't run pictures, but get the story out—general descriptions, ages, sizes. It just could be that somebody would come wandering in and say, my cousin's next-door neighbor had kids like that, or, a girl friend of mine babysat with some kids like that—you never did know, and you had to do what you could on one like this.

He decided to talk to Goulding again. If he could make any guesses about backgrounds—Caucasian, Latin, whatever—probably no dental work to record. He got up and went downstairs. As he passed the desk where Sergeant Bill Dick was sitting in on Duff's day off, a woman was leaning on the counter talking to him, a tall white-haired woman looking upset. People usually were upset about something when they came into a police station.

Varallo got up at the usual time because of the heat wave. There was a lot of work to do on his roses, and he wanted to get most of it done before the worst of the heat; it had gone up to

ninety-seven yesterday. He had got Alida Lovett well sprayed
for the aphids, and on general principles sprayed all the other
climbers—he couldn't do everything at once—and was scientif-
ically measuring the latest rose food he was trying, when Laura
looked into the garage.

"Vic, do you mind if I take the Gremlin? I shouldn't be
later than noon, if I don't have to wait at the doctor's—and
I've got just a few things to pick up at the market. I could take
the baby over to Mrs. Anderson if you're awfully busy—"

"Don't fuss, *cara*. I'll keep an eye on her. We'll have to save
up to buy you one too."

"It's so much easier to park," said Laura. She brought their
very best baby out to her playpen in the shade at the side of
the house, and handed Gideon to Varallo to hold while she
backed out—Gideon, otherwise an astute feline, had no caution
about cars.

Varallo spread rose food methodically, starting with the beds
nearest the house and working toward the fence. He was anxious
to see that Pedrálbes bloom: a chartreuse rose should be interesting. Charlotte Armstrong and Olé were blooming strongly. His
first love when the unlikely hobby had seized him, Duquesa de
Peñeranda, was doing nicely, and Neige Parfum had never
looked back after a slow start.

There were aphids just showing on Mandalay, Lady Margaret
Stewart, and Lowell Thomas. Varallo swore, going back for the
spray can and checking on the baby on the way.

An hour later, taking a breather over a Coke in the patio, he
got to wondering about Katz. When he finished the Coke he
went in and called the station.

"Bill? How's Joe, do you know? We got into a little ruction
yesterday—"

"Yeah, I heard about it," said Sergeant Dick. "We're a little
busy here, but I just talked to him—"

"Listed," Katz had said thickly, "I won't be id for a while.
Tell the lieutenant."

"O.K. What's up?"

"The doctor wadts to take sobe X rays, see if it's broked. I'll be id about eleven, udless it is. It feels as if it is," said Katz.

"All right, I'll pass it on." Sergeant Dick put the phone down and turned back to the woman. "If you can show me some identification, ma'am, and authorize us to do that—if you really think it's necessary—"

"Yes," she said. "Yes, I do. I told you"—she offered him her opened billfold, driver's license uppermost—"I really am his mother. I ought to know him, Sergeant. He's just like his father— old slow and steady, all business, that's Barney. Just like Harry. He always calls me every day, nearly—both the boys do, since I've been alone. Good boys. And he hasn't since last Friday— and I haven't been able to get him, I didn't call his office until yesterday and he wasn't there and they said they didn't know anything about—and that's not like Barney. And Rich hasn't heard from him either, my other son. I wouldn't have had to bother you but I haven't got a key to his apartment, he had the lock changed because there've been burglaries in the neighborhood. I know he's only twenty-eight, but he could be too sick to reach the phone, or fallen—I think we'd better go and look. Rich was going to meet me here—he said it was funny but he didn't really think—"

"You just take it easy, Mrs. Loomis," said Sergeant Dick. "I'll call up a squad car."

Goulding had been unhelpful; he couldn't make any guesses at national backgrounds, except that the kids were white. O'Connor, swearing, had sat down to draft a description based on the meager facts they had, for release to the media. He always had a fight with that infernal machine the typewriter, and when he surfaced some time later he was liberally dabbed with black ink. He ripped the sheets from the roller and saw that Poor had come back and was on the phone.

"Look, this seems to be a thing," said Poor three minutes later, putting the phone down. "A very funny thing. I saw this school nurse—Hoover High. She was in a tizzy about this girl, Rosalie Keating—girl fainted in her first class, and the nurse said she was bleeding pretty badly so she called an ambulance. And then us, because she thought the girl had been raped. Couldn't get anything out of her, but that's what she thought. Well, it didn't sound—you know teen-agers these days—"

"These amoral days," said O'Connor, his deep voice sardonic.

"Yeah. Boy friend just initiated her last night."

"Uh-uh," said Poor. "I was just talking to the doctor down at emergency. She was raped—very forcible rape, he said, within the last ten to twelve hours."

"I'll be damned," said O'Connor. "What's she say about it? I suppose they asked her."

"Nothing. The nurse couldn't get any answers either. And how the hell," asked Poor, "do we question a fifteen-year-old about it, I ask you? The nurse says she's shy. Shy! If she wouldn't talk to the nurse—but the nurse is a tough old battle-ax and maybe wasn't so tactful—"

"Jesus!" said O'Connor suddenly. "Could it be our X with the hangup on Maggie? Another one? I seem to remember, about the same interval between the first two. What's the family like, other kids, house, apartment?"

"I don't know. This just turned into something ten minutes ago."

"So let's find out," said O'Connor.

"Look, I just had a little idea," said Poor. "Maybe a brainstorm. There are times I can see women cops might come in handy—pity we don't have any. But there's this meter maid I've run into a few times at that new short-order stand round the corner. Virginia Waters. She's a nice girl, damn sensible girl, and it just occurs to me, if we got her to talk to this kid—"

"It's an idea. Let's see what you get first. At least you aren't as apt to scare her as me," said O'Connor ungrammatically, grinning at Poor. John Poor didn't look like a big, tough cop, but a nice gentlemanly fellow, slim and sandy and clean-cut.

Tracy and Kogan happened to be the Traffic men Sergeant Dick called in on it. It was an apartment house on Grandview Drive, a fairly new building, not very big—maybe ten apartments.

The woman, Mrs. Loomis, had followed the squad car up there in her own car. She told them it was the rear apartment, on the right. The neatly typed slip in the nameplate said B. J. LOOMIS. There was a new double lock, a second one above the keyhole in the knob.

"Please, just get it open however you can," she said. "Break the door if you have to."

Tracy tried a picklock, but as he suspected there was a deadbolt. He stood back and aimed a hard kick below the knob. He had to hit it four times before the door gave with a loud crack and he and Kogan went in.

"Christ!" said Kogan softly. They saw that first, the body sprawled on the floor in the middle of the living room, and Tracy went to look closer.

"Something for the front office, Bob. His skull's battered in."

And then the woman, coming up behind them, began to scream.

# FOUR

The nurse told Poor he could have five minutes with Rosalie, and led him into a four-bed ward. Rosalie was in the bed nearest the window, with the white curtain drawn on two sides.

"Hello, Rosalie. My name's Poor, I'm a police officer, and I'd like to ask you just a couple of questions." He wasn't sure just how to approach her. His own two kids were a lot younger, and about the only teen-agers he'd had much to do with were the ones on the wrong side, the defiant ones, the sad ones, the misled ones, on dope, in trouble of their own making. By what he'd heard from that school nurse, this one was supposed to be a nice kid.

She turned her head slowly and looked at him briefly before she turned her face to the window again. She didn't look fifteen: still childish, with a round baby face, pale blue eyes under sandy lashes, straight light-brown hair, pale complexion. But the sheet was folded back, and even in the rough hospital gown he could see she had feminine curves, budding young breasts that curiously made her look all the more childish—more vulnerable, he thought suddenly.

"Go away," she said in a thin voice. "I told everybody, nothing's wrong. Nothing happened."

"Well, the doctor thinks something did. And if somebody hurt you, we'd like to know about it, Rosalie, so we can stop him hurting somebody else. Look, if you don't want to talk to me, if you'd tell your mother, or the nurse—"

She just lay there, and the childish, thin mouth formed a hard line, compressed. "There isn't anything to tell anybody."

"And there isn't any reason to be scared," said Poor gently. "If you'll just tell us how it happened—"

She wouldn't look at him, kept her head turned away, and her voice was hard. "I told Mom—there's nothing, nothing happened. Go away—I don't want to talk to you."

That was all he could get out of her. He went out to the hall, and O'Connor was waiting, smoking, in the little alcove with a built-in bench and table. "Evidently the mother's been here," said Poor. "She said something. She's just a kid, and I think scared as hell about something—she won't open up."

"That's the mother." O'Connor nodded down the hall, where a woman was talking to one of the nurses at the station where another hall crossed. "Could be a lot of reasons, John. With a kid. But I'd like to hear something to say yes or no whether it was this same boy, our Maggie Walters boy." He was watching the woman; now she turned and came up the hall, and looked from Poor to O'Connor.

"The nurse said you were police—Lieutenant O'Connor?"

"I'm O'Connor. Detective Poor. Mrs. Keating? Can you tell us anything about this?"

"I wish I could," she said. "It's—out of the blue. They called me—the hospital—for permission to treat her. Rosalie. I couldn't—I can't believe this. It's crazy." She sat down suddenly on the bench and opened her bag, got out a cigarette. O'Connor sat down beside her and offered her a light. "But they said—that doctor—last night. It just couldn't be. It's crazy. Rosalie—and police asking—" She looked at O'Connor with more attention.

"Does she have a boy friend?" asked O'Connor casually.

She shook her head. She was an attractive woman, about thirty-five, dark-haired with a milky complexion, fine dark eyes; she was quietly well dressed in navy and white, her make-up discreet, her nails uncolored. "She hasn't got up any interest yet, which is fine with me. I suppose you could say she's young for her age. Look, Lieutenant, doctors can be wrong. I—we've got a good relationship, Rosalie and I—she wouldn't be afraid to tell me anything. I can't help thinking—she always has some difficulty with her periods, and it could be just that—"

"The doctor doesn't think so."

"But it's impossible!" she exclaimed blankly. "He said last night, and it just couldn't be! She was home all evening, just doing her homework—"

"Were you there?"

"No, I was out. But I know she was! She was sound asleep when I came in at about eleven-thirty—"

"From a date?"

"Yes," she said, putting out the cigarette. She was reacting inevitably to his very masculine aura, looking at him with more interest; her tone was sharp. "I've been divorced since Rosalie was three—there are a couple of men I date now and then. I went out to dinner with Ken Butler—Howie Thurstan had called but I'd set up the date with Ken, I—you're not interested in that. The point is, Rosalie was asleep in bed when I came in. If anything had happened she'd have—"

"You don't know she hadn't been out," said O'Connor. "You have an apartment—a house? She have a key?"

"Yes, an apartment on Dryden Street. Yes, of course she has a key—I work at Hornblower and Weekes downtown. But you don't understand—she's so young for her age, she's shy, she wouldn't—sneak, Lieutenant. Not like that."

"It's a funny age," said O'Connor, "as we both know. The doctor says rape. Now in spite of what you think, Mrs. Keating, it could be she went out to meet some boy and he, um, took advantage of her, and she's too scared and shocked to tell. But it could also be that somehow she ran into something else. When you came home last night, was the door locked? Intact—didn't look as if it had been forced?"

"Well, of course not," she said, staring. "Yes, it was locked. Rosalie knows it should always be locked when she's there alone."

"We know there's a rapist running around town lately," said

O'Connor. "We'd just like to know what happened there, if this could tie up to a couple of other cases."

"A—but this whole thing is just crazy," she said. "Rosalie! She's always been truthful—a good girl. She told me nothing happened, it's just her period. And you and the doctor saying— I just don't know what to think." She looked at them a little wildly. "You want me to talk to her—keep asking her. Well, all I can say is, I want to know too—if anything did happen. But why on earth wouldn't she tell *me*? It just doesn't seem possible—I know my own girl, and she just wouldn't *sneak*."

"We'd appreciate hearing anything she does tell you. And we'll probably want to talk to her again. Thanks very much." O'Connor stood up.

"But it's crazy. Just—she was late getting off to school this morning, but I saw her leave—we left about the same time, she was just the same as always, she kissed me good-by and said have a good day and—oh, my Lord, this is about the last thing I ever expected. Yes, I understand, Lieutenant. I'll talk to her and we'll see." She went back down the hall, her back stiff.

"And you know," said Poor, "even though she seems like a sensible woman, mothers don't always know everything about daughters. Especially teen-age daughters. I don't think this ties up with our X. More likely you guessed it right—she went out to meet some boy from school."

"All the symptoms," agreed O'Connor. "But it'd be nice to know for sure. Look at what we do know, John. She was in the apartment alone. And the three cases we've tied up to the Maggie Walters boy, he's broken in so quick and quiet nobody heard anything, got hold of those women before they could scream or fight him. So, Mrs. Keating says the door was locked when she came home, not forced. Was it locked all evening? There's just an outside chance—"

"If the girl won't come apart, I don't see how we'll ever know. When she wouldn't tell the mother—"

"She may yet," said O'Connor.

At the station, Wayne was taking a statement from the owner of the furniture store; nobody else was there. He sauntered over, seeing them come in, and said, "We've now got a new homicide. Jeff went out on it and I chased Joe out when he came in. All I heard, it looks like another offbeat thing."

"They do say, Satan finds work for idle hands," said O'Connor. "Where is it? I'd better go and look at it."

Grandview Avenue was in a settled substantial residential area, zoned for apartments. The address was just down from a block-long shopping area; the mobile lab unit was parked outside, and Katz's Olds. O'Connor found a slot for the Ford and walked back; it was an open-plan place, built around a central paved patio with a small pool, and once in he could hear the voices from the rear, and drifted back there. The apartment door was open, and he went in.

"I wondered when you'd show up," said Katz. He was wearing a bandage across the bridge of his nose, which gave him a slightly rakish air. Burt was kneeling across the room dusting the edge of a coffee table; Forbes and Katz had been talking to another man who stood against the wall smoking nervously. They gravitated over to O'Connor. "So far, nothing much shows —we just got here." Katz filled him in on the background: family couldn't contact young Loomis lately, which was unusual, and his mother came over from Hollywood, asked police to break in.

"That's the older brother," said Forbes. "He got here before we did. The old lady was all to pieces, he called a cab and sent her to his place, said his wife'd look after her. He's Richard Loomis, attorney with an address in West L.A. Very respectable citizen—as we gather the dead man was. Barnard J. Loomis, twenty-eight. All we know at the moment."

For the moment O'Connor ignored Loomis. He went across and looked at the dead man lying quietly in the middle of the living-room floor. He was a stocky, barrel-chested young man with regular features, a strong nose, square chin, broad forehead, thick dark hair. He was wearing navy slacks and a sleeve-less undershirt, a rather elegant navy shantung dressing gown over those, lying loose around him. He was on his back, arms flung out, and he'd bled a little at the mouth. He wasn't just recently dead, O'Connor saw at a glance; the doctor would say how long, but at a guess several days at least. But there was an air-conditioning unit going; that could make a difference in hot weather.

He squatted over the corpse and reached gently to the black-ened bruise at the left temple. Definite depression—maybe all that had done the trick, one blow. He stood up and looked around.

"Look—do we have to stay in here? I'd just as soon—" Richard Loomis cleared his throat. "I know this is—just a job to you, but he's my brother, and this just—it makes no sense, I'm still trying to believe it."

"Suppose we go out to the patio, sir," suggested Katz. "No-body else around."

"Yes. No—I think most of the tenants here are away at work all day—except for the Lundgrens, they live next to Barney—old couple—could be they heard something—"

O'Connor looked at the dead man again, and Burt said, "I've printed it, but keep your paws off it—I'll pack it up in a minute—but that could be the weapon."

"I noticed it," said O'Connor. It lay a couple of feet up from the corpse's head, a heavy glass bookend, solid and square. He couldn't see any mark on it, but maybe the microscope could. He looked around for the mate and found it on the top shelf of the bookcase inside the front door. It was a nice apart-ment, obviously a man's place. This room was a good size with two wide windows in two walls, one looking out on the patio: open-weave drapes in brown tones, a big brown leather chair, a leather couch, a couple of smaller chairs, a color TV in one corner. It was all very neat and clean: the only sign of disorder was the corpse, a very faint film of dust on a few surfaces. Through a little archway was a neat and clean kitchen with a small table and two chairs at the living-room end: no dirty dishes in the sink, no evidence of recent use. The other door in the living room led to a small, square bedroom, also very orderly. The double bed was made up, with a brown corduroy bedspread. There was a chest, a taller chiffonier, a walk-in closet with orderly rows of clothes. On top of the chiffonier, in a leather tray, were a man's gold wrist watch, a handful of loose change, a black leather billfold. The watch had stopped— O'Connor squinted at it—at eight twenty-five. The door opposite the closet led into a small, neat bathroom. He didn't touch anything; Burt hadn't been in here yet.

He went out to the patio. Loomis was sitting in one of the metal chairs beside the pool, head in hands. It was very hot in the unshaded patio, and the sun was reflected from the too-blue water in a bright glare.

"You know we have to ask questions, Mr. Loomis. I'm Lieutenant O'Connor."

"Yes. All right," said Loomis. "I—this just seems impossible, that's all. Barney. I mean, there are people—things happen to. He wasn't one like that. I don't know if you know what I mean." He lifted his head slowly.

"Wasn't he?" said O'Connor. "Well, that's something for a start." Loomis was a distinguished-looking fellow, about thirty-five, tall, lean, shoulders a little stooped; there was an elusive resemblance to the corpse, but he was better-looking. He was a little foppishly tailored in fawn and brown sports clothes, a massive gold wrist watch and a ring on his left little finger. He looked at O'Connor now and O'Connor, who saw more than most people expected, saw the inevitable judgment in Loomis' eyes: the expectable insensitive tough cop.

Katz and Forbes hung around quietly, listening. "The family were all on good terms with him? You saw each other fairly often?"

"Yes, certainly. That—that was why Mother got worried. Barney and I both call to check on her every day or so. We usually had—my wife and I, I mean—had Barney and Mother to dinner once a week or so. My—our sister Anne lives in Portland."

"When did you see him last?"

"I *saw* him last, last Wednesday night—a week ago today—but I talked to him Friday. About seven. I wanted his opinion"—Loomis stubbed out one cigarette and immediately lit another—"about an investment. Yes, well, maybe that would—tell you more about Barney. He was younger than me, but he had a very good head for money—for—for facts. I'd asked him about it on Wednesday, he said he wanted to think about it before he said anything pro or con. That—that was Barney. Old slow and sure, Mother always called him. He was—steady. You know? Steady. He'd never do anything you wouldn't expect him to. I'm sorry, that's badly put, but—"

"Yes. He had a job here?"

"He was with C. P. Adrian—the tax accountants—ever since he got out of the university. He was a C.P.A., of course."

"Not married. Was he ever?"

"No. No, Barney was never much of a one for chasing around. Or—chasing period."

"Did he have any women friends at all? Even casual?"

"Not that I know of. No. I—it was his own business, but Anne's always teasing him about it, when was he going to get married and so on. I don't know, I—my wife says he's a bachelor by nature. Fussy about his clothes and—"

"Men friends? He have any hobbies, interests outside his job?"

"Chess, he liked to play chess. He could always beat me—I can't play that game. He belonged to a club. Yes, of course he had friends—people we know—family friends—I couldn't say any very close."

"What about enemies?"

"Oh, don't be stupid," said Loomis wearily. "People don't have. People like—Barney never had any trouble with anyone. Arguments, fights—that's stupid. He was just a quiet young fellow with—a quiet little hobby—good at his job."

"Quiet," said O'Connor. "Where was this club he belonged to?"

"What? Oh, it's not that kind of club. They did it by mail—chess players all over the country—white to play and mate in four moves," said Loomis vaguely. "This just isn't a thing that happens—Barney getting killed. The last man. Who in hell would have any reason to kill Barney? Who in *hell?*"

"That's what we'll try to find out," said O'Connor. "We'll be talking to you again, Mr. Loomis." An elderly couple had just come into the patio from the street, and stared at the evidence of activity, the strange men. Loomis said dully, "That's the Lundgrens, I've met them. They live in the next apartment. Barney'd lived here since he got the job in Glendale." Katz moved forward to talk to them; after a few minutes they went on to their own door, reluctant, casting glances back. O'Connor went to talk to Katz.

"N.G. They never heard anything from Mr. Loomis' apartment, he never gave parties—sometimes had his family for dinner, a couple of friends, that's all. They're shocked as all get out," said Katz. "A very nice young man, very much the gentleman, very quiet, very polite. Are you thinking what I'm thinking?"

"Cops tend to have low, suspicious minds—if not to start with, as soon as they're experienced cops. But I don't know, Joe. If he was a fag, I think the family would know—anyway suspected. And when he didn't go out much, or have men coming here—" O'Connor ruminated. "It comes back to people, doesn't it? Some men are just made that way, the natural loners. And it could be too, to go all Freudian, whatever little sex-drive he had was homo only he never did anything about it."

"True," said Katz. "Anyway, what we've heard, he doesn't seem a very likely subject for Murder One. Who felt that strong about him?"

O'Connor sighed. "Well, we may turn up some physical evidence. Find out who saw him last, and— Why wasn't he missed at his job? Or was he? Or did he call in sick, so nobody wondered? And if so, why?"

"And I'll add a thought to that," said Forbes. "Anybody can change his pattern. It could be he'd just fallen for a girl—taken to gambling. Anything."

"If so, something should show somewhere," said O'Connor. "I think I'll go ask questions at C. P. Adrian. After lunch."

After some ruminating on it, Poor still thought his little idea was a good one. That meter maid, Virginia Waters. Girl, he'd said, but she'd be around thirty, he thought, and she was married, with a couple of kids. He might not know much about teen-agers, but he could imagine that a shy, sensitive one like Rosalie—young for her age—might conceivably be too ashamed, or too embarrassed, to tell her mother about a thing like that, even when they had a good relationship. But a sympathetic woman, younger than her mother, a stranger who wouldn't show alarm or indignation or disapproval—she might open up to a calm, friendly approach like that.

The meter maids, riding around in their little open carts checking the parking lots, were not trained policewomen, just police employees; but they were on the same hours as the day watch, he thought. He called the desk to check. This was Virginia Waters' day off. He asked for and got her home phone number, and thought he'd talk to Mrs. Keating about it first.

Wayne had given him the list of loot from the furniture store to get out on the hot list to pawnbrokers. "Probably a waste of time. It was a slick pro job, and they didn't touch anything they couldn't fence right off. Adding machines, tape recorders, portable TVs. I'd take no bets they left us any latents. I dusted here and there, but I'll be surprised if anything shows."

"Wasn't there a burglar alarm, place like that?"

Wayne grinned, stretching and flexing his muscles. "Sure there was. The owner's brother-in-law installed it to save him money. All very professional, rigged to alert us the minute it was set off. They'd covered all three doors and all five windows, and never thought about the skylight. That's how they got in, and cut the wires on the alarm before they went out the door.

They, I say, because the amount of stuff gone says at least
two."

"People, people," said Poor. "So maybe it was some employee
there who happened to notice that?"

"Too complicated," said Wayne. "The slick pro job. Just taking a chance, and not such a long chance at that. It's funny
how often skylights do get overlooked, even by the supposed
experts. We'll have a look in records for any of the punks who
go in for that sort of stuff, and go and lean on them. Just
another routine job."

Forbes and Katz came in after lunch, and relayed the background on the new homicide. "There was an address book,"
said Forbes, producing it. "It's been printed. Charles said we'd
better talk to everybody in it, checking for who saw him last,
whether he said anything to anybody that might give us a
lead. If you ask me, Joe called this one down on us, saying we
were due for the offbeat ones. I suppose there could be some
simple answer, but on the face of it, it's just funny. The last
man, as the brother said. And it wasn't just the casual break-in,
because the brother said nothing's missing from the place."

The addresses were scattered from Pasadena to Beverly Hills,
but the brother had identified most of them: people known
to the family. Upright, respectable people; they could be checked
by phone, no need to go running all over to talk to them
personally. And it didn't sound as if they'd get anything anyway, said Katz pessimistically. "Just what the brother said about
him, that kind I know. Close-mouthed. If he was having any
trouble with anybody, any money worries, nobody'd have
heard—he'd never talk about it. Of course, money—there's always a motive in money. I'm going to have a look at his bank
record."

Just about then, however, an autopsy report came in: on that
queer one Monday night, the citizen dropping dead in front of
Rhys and Hunter. One Alfred Reinhart, fifty-nine. He hadn't

had a heart attack or a stroke; he'd died of a skull fracture inflicted probably within an hour of death.

"Well, that'll be a little shock for that drunk," said Poor. "Did we ever find out who he is?"

They had. He'd been held in the tank that night, and warned to appear at the court hearing on the 502 citation, and turned loose. He was listed as Peter Selby of an address on Geneva. The inquest on Reinhart was scheduled for Friday.

One of the frustrations of police work was that something new was always coming up. Now Wayne set the machinery going for a warrant on Selby, and Katz went out to see if he could pick him up, while Forbes went to the bank to have a look at Loomis' account.

The address on Geneva was an old bastard-Spanish stucco house with a beautiful dichondra lawn in front. Katz, who had once spent a frustrating few years trying to get one to grow, eyed it with respect. He'd had a look in records for Selby: he had a whole string of arrests for common drunkenness, and his next of kin was listed as a married daughter at the same address, so Katz deduced that the daughter had a gardening husband.

"Mrs. Durkin?" He showed the badge as the door was opened. "Detective Katz, headquarters. I'm looking for Mr. Peter Selby."

"Oh, my lord," she said in exasperation. "I might have known he was lying. Said somebody ran into the car when he was parked. I might have known. He had an accident, didn't he? And you found out his license is suspended permanently." She was comfortably plump, ordinarily good-humored, about fifty.

"Well, we did notice that. Is he here?"

"He is. In the patio. I've got the best Christian husband the Lord ever made, Mr. Katz, and he's got the patience of a saint, but that was the last straw, when Dad took the car on Monday. Four hundred and seventy dollars the garage said, and Jim got mad for once, read Dad the riot act. I guess we'll have to hide the keys from now on." She was leading him through an unpretentious house, down a long hall, to a side door onto a paved patio. "I wonder if a policeman like you could explain it—if you see a lot of that kind of thing."

"What's that?"

She stopped with her hand on the door. "Well, it seems funny to me, because it was all of a sudden. He used—all the time up to when my mother died—he worked a regular job, steady as could be, used to take a drink now and then but never more than one or two. And then after Ma died, he went off the rails all at once and started to get drunk." She shook her head. "It's funny."

"They were pretty close maybe? He missed her—felt lonely."

"Well, I don't know. They fought like cat and dog for forty years. Dad? Here's a police officer to see you. You told us a lie about the car, you had an accident, didn't you, and maybe hurt somebody, and now—oh, my Lord, I expect it'll be a big fine, won't it?" She looked at Katz, stricken. "He's only got the Social Security, and if it was an awful lot I don't know how we'd—"

"Ah, Millie," said the old man. "I'm sorry, Millie." He was a mild-looking old fellow, not very big, paunchy and bald, with a freckled skin and faded blue eyes. He'd been sitting in the shade in an old wicker rocker, reading the *Herald*; he had on a very clean pair of old overalls and a bright red shirt.

"Is it a big fine, for what he did?"

"Well, a little something more. You see, Mr. Selby, that man whose car you ran into—you had a fight with him, you remember that? Before the officers brought you into the station?"

"I guess I did. He started it. I never meant to run into him. He hit me so I hit him back."

"And knocked him down and fractured his skull," said Katz gently, "and he's dead, Mr. Selby."

"Dead? Well, do tell. I sure never meant to hurt him none. I didn't even know him. Just a little punch like that, he's dead?"

"I'm afraid so. You'll have to come with me—it'll be a charge of manslaughter."

"Oh, my dear Lord!" said the woman. "What Jim will say! Manslaughter! And a lawyer and all—oh, my dear Lord!"

O'Connor came back to the station at four-fifty, muttering and uneasy. He wished Varallo was there to talk it over with: fill Varallo in tomorrow, see what he thought. Varallo got the nuances, their handsome blond Eytie; so did O'Connor, but they didn't always come to the surface explicitly right away. All he was thinking now was, there was something fishy at C. P. Adrian.

Whatever it was, it wasn't C. P. Adrian himself. A delicate, frail-looking fellow in the sixties, probably tough as whalebone, and clear as glass—an honest man, obviously sincere. Talking like something out of Dickens.

"Oh, dear me, dear me." A kind of agitated squeak. "Dead? Barney Loomis dead? But how—why—when? Only a young man —such a very reliable man—such a steady fellow—this is terrible, terrible!" He wasn't twentieth century. But he must know his business; that was a solid accountancy firm, good reputation, a fixture right there on Glendale's main drag for twenty years.

He said he hadn't realized Loomis hadn't been in this week. Well, he had a private office, and an outfit like that, it could be everything was so well organized, ran along so smooth, the boss wouldn't necessarily miss one man. Four other men in a big outer office divided up into cubicles, four or five girls around: stenographic pool. Adrian could have thought, Loomis out on a break, not seeing him. But the rest of them—

O'Connor pulled his tie loose and lit a cigarette and muttered swear-words to himself, and Wayne, eying him, refrained from asking questions. The rest of them? Those girls. Exactly the kind of girls—fluffy, pretty little curvaceous good-time chicks —Charles O'Connor used to go chasing, before he fell for his Katy who really wasn't his type at all, only an inch shorter and so damned thin . . . before the baby . . . and at least she didn't wear high heels now. But the rest of them in that office —and not one damned thing to put a finger on, because, damn it, it was natural, in a way. People being people. And it was June, not as if they'd had a spate of business, everybody's damn taxes to figure up at once, so a man would be missed . . . but all the same it was just a little peculiar . . .

"I thought you were interested," said Burt loudly.

O'Connor jumped. "What?"

"On this thing. On the baby. I did the best I could with it," said Burt. "It's surprising what infrared can show up, but I hoped I'd get it clearer. More of it. Still, it is something. May give us somewhere to go." He wanted some appreciation for a difficult job. O'Connor sat up.

"You got something on that?"

"See what you think." Burt produced a photographic print, still a trifle damp. It was an eight-by-ten, on fine-grain stock, and the subject was very fuzzy. It looked like a surrealistic study of a dog collar. Burt offered him a large magnifying glass with a built-in battery light. "Take a real close look."

O'Connor switched on the fluorescent desk lamp and adjusted the print under it, moved the glass up and down, and suddenly said, "I will be goddamned! I will be—when I saw that damned thing I thought Goulding was really reaching. I couldn't have said what the hell it was—"

"That's what it was," said Burt. "It gives us something." And the article with the kids' descriptions would be in tonight's *Herald*, tomorrow's *Times*; but this could be a good deal more helpful.

Just a little more. The oblique light, the infrared, hadn't brought out all there might have been, and it took the great enlargement, the magnifying glass, to make it legible, even blurred; but there it was. The little typed letters from that darker square on the decayed plastic, all the letters that could be deciphered. "LDMAN," said O'Connor. "That what you read?"

"And maybe another N at the end. I'm sorry I couldn't bring up any more. But I'd read that as part of a name, and most likely a surname. Not the hospital's name. It's not much, but it gives us a handle, maybe."

"Very much maybe. But thanks, Rex—that's a nice piece of work." But when Burt had gone back to the lab, pleased with himself, O'Connor took a second look and felt pessimistic. A handle? To identify those kids? So, a baby bracelet from the hospital left on the baby—and on it a partial surname, just possibly. It could be from a hospital anywhere in the fifty states. And what a hunt.

He took it over to show Wayne. "And you know something else, Charles," said Wayne. "We can't just call all the hospitals in L. A. County and say, please check your records. For any female babies born—when?"

"Doctors can be wrong. Goulding said under six months. Give it leeway. Call it between last November and March."

"Yeah. Between last November and March, with a surname ending LDMAN. You know we'll have to go look personally— hospitals are busy places, they wouldn't have time to paw over all those files. And how many hospitals there are even just in L. A. County—and while it isn't as if it was Smith or Jones, I suppose there are a good many names ending LDMAN—and nothing says it was a hospital here or in New York or Hawaii."

"I know, I know," said O'Connor. "But it's a place to start. At least." Wayne agreed dispiritedly.

When O'Connor got home, fighting his way in the gate with Maisie leaping at him frenziedly and shouting to the world that Master had come, Katharine was shredding lettuce at the sink.

"Roquefort or blue cheese? Yes, I'm fine. And Mary Lou McNally called. The new obedience class is starting on July 2, you told her you'd take Maisie."

"Oh hell, who has time?" said O'Connor. "Listen, I know she ought to be trained, but it takes enough time getting her out for exercise weekends—"

"She'd be a good deal more manageable," said Katharine amusedly.

"Well, I'll think about it," said O'Connor.

# FIVE

When Poor got home on Wednesday night he found a note from his wife: she'd taken the children to a Disney matinee and they might be a little late. Philosophically Poor poured himself a glass of sherry; secretly he was rather ashamed of liking that genteel wine. He decided to try Virginia Waters' phone number again, and this time got her, and explained. She was interested and sympathetic.

"Of course I'd be glad to try, Mr. Poor. The poor kid—I think you might be right there, even if she's close to her mother, she might talk to somebody else easier. Is she still in the hospital?"

Poor had checked. "She'll be released in the morning. The mother works, and I gather Rosalie's O.K. to be alone. I'll talk to Mrs. Keating, of course."

"Well, I'll be glad to have a try at it, if I can get somebody to change with me—Nella probably would, and it's her day off. I'll let you know, Mr. Poor." Her warm voice raised her image in his mind: not exactly pretty, but nice, a buxom dark young woman, outgoing and friendly.

He didn't try to get Mrs. Keating until later, after they'd had dinner and got the kids to bed. When he spoke his name Mrs. Keating hesitated and then said, "Oh, yes. At the hospital. You were the other one. I beg your pardon—" Poor grinned, unoffended; he thought most men would be remembered as the other one alongside Charles O'Connor. He explained.

"Oh," she said. "Well, it's quite all right with me, if it's a policewoman. I see the sense in that—Rosalie might talk to someone like that. No. I haven't tried to—she's been so tense and wound up, I didn't like to prod her. Yes, she's all right physically, they said—but that's the least of it. I'm keeping her in bed, but I'll have to go to work tomorrow. Should I tell her about this woman?"

"Let's play it by ear," said Poor.

"Well, all right." She sounded pretty tense and wound up herself, he thought.

On Thursday morning, when Varallo came in O'Connor was poring over a sheaf of glossy eight-by-ten photographs. "Sit down and hear about our new homicide, Vic. I want you to go sniff round at it—you and your ESP—and tell me who did it, why." Katz had wandered in after Varallo, and O'Connor thrust the photographs over to them. "You remind me if I forget to tell him anything, Joe. Now look, here's this quiet young bachelor, a loner, good job, good family, and never known to have trouble with anybody—" He sketched in the background rapidly.

"Burt did some overtime, getting these prints out," said Katz. "Kind of brings it home to you how funny it looked. That nice neat apartment, just the corpse."

"Now you can see"— O'Connor stabbed his blunt forefinger at the photographs Varallo was looking at—"there wasn't any struggle there. We can deduce this and that. His brother talked to him on the phone about seven Friday night. We haven't talked to everybody he knew—Fred can do some phoning around on that today—"

"Hey," said Wayne, "I've got some legwork to do on this break-in."

"—And we haven't heard what Goulding has to say about probable time of death. He could have been killed Friday, Saturday, or Sunday, who knows? I think he must have been dead by Sunday, because he didn't show up for work on Monday. But what it looks like, it was sometime in the evening—he'd come home, from work or wherever, and got partly undressed—maybe had a meal out or fixed himself something then, and cleaned up the kitchen—when he had a visitor. Somebody he let in. We can guess the visitor didn't come planning to kill him, because of that glass bookend—probably that's what he was hit with. It was the only thing out of place in that damned apartment."

"I can see," said Varallo thoughtfully, studying the photographs. "Very natty young gent, him and his silk dressing gown. Very nice furniture. You said a loner?"

"Well, damn it," said O'Connor, "that's another thing. After I'd talked to those people at his office, I thought, something funny—but was it? Eight other people there—other accountants, stenos—and they all seem to be chummy together—but this Loomis, Vic, he wasn't thirty yet but all we've heard about him, he acted like sixty. He'd worked there six, seven years—"

"Where?"

"Adrian tax agency on Brand. But he didn't mingle, he wasn't the hail fellow well met. So maybe it wasn't so funny that nobody bothered to check up on him when he didn't show on Monday. We don't know what Burt might turn up in physical evidence, but the type Loomis was, it doesn't seem likely anybody'd have had a grudge on him. I haven't seen what Jeff turned up at the bank yesterday"—this was Forbes's day off—"but he'd have been making good money there. Fifteen, eighteen thousand—plenty for a single man. The born bachelor. The chess player. Didn't go out much, didn't have people in. And nobody," added O'Connor, "heard anything from his apartment all weekend. I went back and asked, when people were home last night. No shouts or screams or dull thuds. I want you to take a look at that office. Vic. Was it funny they didn't check up on him? Maybe I'm reading too much into it."

Varallo lit a cigarette. "For the crude, tough cop, Charles, you sometimes have the valid hunches. I wouldn't say I'm that much smarter, but I'll have a look. The lab may give us the whole answer, or something show in the bank record."

"Sometimes," said Katz darkly, "the lab can give us too much. You haven't seen Burt's masterpiece. That'll make legwork from now till Christmas."

Varallo heard about that interestedly. "Ingenious," he said sardonically, "and funny. The baby bracelet. But if you think it's going to get those bodies identified hey presto, you're grasping at straws. The baby could have been born—"

"In New York or Miami, I know," said O'Connor. "All I say is, we have to go on the probabilities. The bodies were dumped up there, in one of the few places I can think of around here where it was unlikely they'd be found. You grant that, damn it? All right, whoever did it must be familiar with the general area. The baby wasn't over six months old or so. The probability is that it was born somewhere around here. And this is a lead to a possible surname, so we'd better follow it up."

"As against that," said Katz mildly, "I'll only point out that the bodies were just dumped, no attempt to bury them—just left up there in plain sight of whoever did come wandering by six months later. So maybe whoever did it didn't care whether they were found. All right, I know we have to work it." Poor had drifted in and stood listening.

"I've got to cover the damn inquest," said O'Connor. "You can start on the hospitals, Joe—you and John try the Adventist, I'll go over to Memorial when I get out of court. And somebody ought to talk to the Loomises again when they're not so upset—say this afternoon. You might go and look at that apartment, Vic—see if you come up with any hunches."

"I'll put more faith in the lab evidence. O.K."

"We may have something out of Rosalie sometime," said Poor. "I got hold of that meter maid."

O'Connor frowned. "The more I think of that, the more I think it's nothing for us at all. Teen-agers. The boy friend a little overanxious, and Rosalie scared. But that's another thing, the damn nut and his Maggie Walters."

"Who is Maggie, what is she," murmured Katz, feeling his nose; he was still wearing the bandage. "There can't be many surnames that end LDMAN—but you do realize that after we've collected any from the hospitals, we then have to go look at the babies? To be sure they're there and not the one dumped up in the hills?"

"Go, go," said O'Connor, and looked at his watch. "Hell, I've got to get to that inquest."

As expected, the coroner gave an open verdict on the bodies of the children: Murder One by X, and O'Connor got away from the court by ten. He'd been surprised and interested at the result Burt had got with that photograph, and it had looked like a good, hot lead on identifying the bodies: but belatedly it was brought home to him what a lot of digging was going to be involved.

These days the computers made short cuts; but they couldn't be programmed to do everything, and some jobs still had to be done the hard way.

He got over to the Memorial Hospital at ten-fifteen, asked for the head of the maternity floor, and explained what he was after. He was sent back downstairs to talk to the accounting office, where a severely efficient, spectacled female told him that all back records were sent to the dead files once every thirty days, and microfilmed every six months. She was quite willing to co-operate, a little pleasantly thrilled by the badge —or O'Connor—but naturally all the staff had their own work to do, if he cared to look at the records himself she'd give him a note to the head custodian.

"You have to take the last elevator at the north end, sir— one level below Therapy and X Ray."

Eventually O'Connor wound up in a big, bare room with a single naked bulb over what looked like an autopsy table and with nowhere to sit but a high stool. The damned hospitals looked so efficient and hygienic on the surface, but he had a suspicion there was just as much muddle below the surface as in most businesses. Moreover, the birth records seemed to be listed by dates, not names; it was nearly noon before he acci- dentally discovered that they were cross-filed under names too.

It was tedious work, pawing through the records of births

for January, February, and March. If he wanted to look back further, he'd have to get them to dig up the microfilms; for the moment he'd take Goulding's word on the baby's age.

The Memorial was a big hospital; a lot of babies had been born here in that three months. When O'Connor realized he was starving, and took a break to go out for some lunch, he'd collected three possible names. Mrs. Jerome Wildman, address in Glendale; female child born January 13. Mrs. William Aldman, La Crescenta, female child born February 12. Mrs. James Tildman, female child born February 24. It was a meager haul; but there were more files to look at.

He went back to them, and by the time he came to the end of March he had just one more: Mrs. Frederick Goldman, Glendale, female child born March 23.

It didn't look like much for most of a day's work. And he'd said probabilities; but people did move around. Say the baby had even been born in Los Angeles: there were dozens of hospitals—"Hell and damnation!" said O'Connor to himself. "Now why did Rex have to work so hard on that photograph?" But you had to follow up what leads you got. And there was the story in the papers: a lot of people should see that in the *Times* today.

He wondered what Poor and Katz were getting at the Adventist.

"So you didn't think of checking to see why Loomis hadn't come in?"

"Why should I? We've all got work to do—oh well, naturally I figured he'd called in sick." Jim Dumbarton gave Varallo an easy smile. "Jesus, that is something—old Loomis getting taken off like that—but the crime rate these days—only you never think it'll happen to you or anybody you know. No, I didn't think much about it, tell the truth, I think Secrist said something, wondered if Loomis had picked up this flu bug, but that's about all."

"I see," said Varallo. He looked around this office. It was

a prosperous-looking office, if not huge: a big, square room with little gates into cubicles for desks, a cluster of typing desks at the front where evidently the four stenographers worked. Four men at four desks back here, and the one empty cubicle and empty desk with the wooden nameplate: B. J. LOOMIS. "He wasn't often off sick?"

"Never knew him to be before," said Dumbarton, and then looked uneasy for some reason.

"You all got along all right? Friendly?"

Dumbarton shrugged and looked away. "Oh, sure. Sure. Well, naturally there isn't much—er—time for chatting, we're all busy. I can't say I knew Loomis awfully well, just another fellow in the office, but he was a nice guy. All business—not the old college pal, but a nice guy." He gave Varallo a frank smile.

"None of you goes out to lunch together, a friendly drink after hours?"

"Oh, my God, Adrian's death on liquor. No, actually I usually go up to that Swedish place, Secrist does too. I think Loomis was a health-food nut, he always went to one of those. Uh—you didn't say—was it a burglar? Broke in and killed him?"

"We're still investigating," said Varallo noncommittally. "Do you each have one special stenographer, or just any one who's free?"

"Oh, turn and turn around, sort of. They're all good girls."

"Well, thanks," said Varallo. Like O'Connor, he felt vaguely dissatisfied with this place, but he couldn't decide why. He had talked to the other men. Adam Secrist, Steve O'Dell, Harry Pace. All men in their thirties, like Dumbarton: all oddly alike outwardly: the new wide-lapel jackets, colored shirts, lobe-length hair, sideburns: this year's version, the youngish business executive, successful, ambitious. They weren't alike, of course: Secrist was short and sandy, Dumbarton was built like a wrestler, O'Dell was a good-looking black Irishman, the winning charm, and Pace was going bald. Dumbarton and Pace wore wedding rings, but they could all be married: not all men did wear rings. They'd all told him much the same things. Loomis a very nice guy, all business, reliable, maybe a little stand-offish, but easy to get along with. They'd all tried to pump him about the murder, but that was natural.

When he drifted down to the stenos' section, he was expected and welcomed; they'd been watching him with the men. He introduced himself, and they asked excited questions. Was Mr. Loomis really dead? Killed? And how, and who? "Somebody you *know*," said the redheaded one. "Mr. Loomis. I mean, anybody can get killed in an accident, but getting murdered —my goodness."

He sorted them out. The redhead was Sally Karpis, the youngest one, about twenty-two. The others all a little older: Carole Mederos, Lynn Newman, Paula Fearn. "You all knew him pretty well?" Varallo laid out conscious charm deliberately, and they responded, pleased with the break in the day, the excitement and drama, and the good-looking blond cop.

"Well, we all *knew* him," said Sally. "Sure. We work for all the men—there's a lot of typing, you know, they always keep us busy. Mr. Loomis—goodness, think of him being dead, killed —he was awfully particular. Liked everything just so."

"Oh? Complained about little mistakes, you mean?"

"You don't make little mistakes, or big ones, in a tax office," said Paula Fearn, "or you don't stay. What's it matter about Loomis being fussy if he's dead? Was it a burglar?"

"We're still investigating. You were all friendly with him, though? No trouble, any arguments?"

"Oh, no," said Sally, round-eyed. "This is a nice place to work. All the men are nice."

"Did Loomis ever throw a pass at any of you? Any of you ever go out with him?"

"Good heavens, no," said Lynn Newman. "We weren't—on those terms. Just like Sally says, the men are all friendly, but— well, we've all got our own friends. I couldn't imagine Mr. Loomis throwing a pass at anybody."

The Mederos girl smiled at Varallo a little maliciously: she was dark and svelte. "He was strictly from Boresville," she said. "Dull his middle name. Quite the gentleman."

"I see," said Varallo. "So—"

"Did you say your name's Varallo? That's Italian, isn't it?"

He wasn't about to waste time explaining about North Italians. "So you didn't do any checking or asking when he didn't come in on Monday." The last time anybody here had seen Loomis was six o'clock last Friday, so they all said.

"I think I asked Mr. Dumbarton if he was sick. He—Mr. Loomis I mean—had asked me especially to have that Trillingham account ready on Monday. Mr. Dumbarton said he probably had the flu, that's all I know. To *think*," said Sally, "of him lying there dead all this time! Was he? Was that why he didn't come in?"

"I figured he'd asked old C.P. for some time off," said Paula, examining her nails. "He was a pet of the old boy's, birds of a feather."

"So you didn't exactly miss him," said Varallo.

Carole laughed. "We were busy. More interesting subjects to talk about on a break than Mr. Old Maid Loomis. Though I must say, if we'd known he was getting killed by a burglar—"

Varallo stood up. "Well, thanks."

"Welcome," said Paula. He felt their eyes on him as he moved away.

He had seen Adrian, who had said fussily that he could look at Loomis' desk provided he didn't remove any of the firm's papers. A search warrant was applied for in case anything turned up here, but Varallo doubted he'd find anything interesting. He didn't. The desk was very neat, not only outside but inside: files of forms, notes, lists of figures, all tidily put away in labeled manila envelopes: all the various accounts Loomis had been responsible for. There was nothing personal there at all except a Parker pen with his name on it and a cigarette lighter in the shape of a carved wooden chessman, a handsome knight.

It wasn't, Varallo reflected, a bizarre murder, not at all: just shapeless, and no handle to grasp on it. Who indeed had felt strongly enough about B. J. Loomis to want him dead?

The man was so colorless . . . Wasting a little more time, Varallo drove up to that apartment on Grandview, broke the police seal on the door, and went in. A man's surroundings often said this and that about him.

This place didn't say much. He had the feeling that B. J. Loomis would have strongly disapproved the mess the cops had left behind, the chalked outline of the body on the brown carpet, the film of dusting powder on the furniture. Otherwise the place was so neat and clean. Between the leather chair and the couch stood a plain pedestal game table, its top inlaid with a chessboard. No chess set visible: Varallo went hunting, didn't find any, and deduced that the pieces had been standing out, and Burt had packed them up for printing.

B. J. Loomis sitting here over a game of chess with somebody who suddenly went berserk at getting checkmated, grabbed the bookend, and biffed him with it?

"*Per carità*," said Varallo to himself, "let's not get carried away here." He looked in the kitchen cupboards. No liquor around anywhere. Packages of health-food cereal: cans of vegetable protein synthetic meat. He wandered back to the living room and looked at the bookcase. There was no fiction at all: a shelf of textbooks on chess, a few books about Yoga, more on nutrition and dietetics—cooking. But strictly from Boresville, thought Varallo. How in hell had the man got himself murdered?

Poor, swearing and struggling through the birth records at the Adventist Hospital—Katz had gone over to the Community —hadn't found any possible names at all by the time he went out for lunch. He called the station to ask if Mrs. Waters had called. She hadn't.

By two o'clock he had found one name. Mrs. Robert Oldman, address in Montrose, female baby born February 2 this year. He found a public phone and called to ask if Mrs. Waters had called. She hadn't. Duff sounded curious, answering.

At three-thirty Poor came trailing tiredly back to the station, feeling that he'd wasted the day. "Your meter maid just called," said Duff. "Left a number."

Feeling slightly better, Poor went up to the office. Nobody else was there. He sat down and dialed the number.

"Oh, Mr. Poor. Virginia Waters. I'm sorry I got delayed on this—I couldn't get off this morning. But you were right about Rosalie. I've got her to open up and talk. I just made it plain to her, the way you said, that the doctors know about it and she had to tell sooner or later, and when it wasn't her fault there wasn't any reason to be ashamed. She's a nice little girl, Mr. Poor, a bit immature."

"Well, that's great," said Poor. "What—"

"What I wanted to ask you—I think she's O.K. for me to bring her in so you can talk to her. She says she's willing, and I thought you'd rather hear it all for yourself so you can ask what you want to."

"You're a miracle worker if you've opened her up that far. Yes, I would."

"Oh, she just wanted explaining to, she's not stupid," said Virginia matter-of-factly. "We'll be down in fifteen minutes."

Wayne came in before that with an unkempt lout to question, and Poor told him to get out, explained. "I want it all nice and quiet here for Rosalie, Fred." Wayne grinned and stashed his captive in an interrogation room, said he'd guard the door, if O'Connor showed up the poor girl would be scared dumb again.

But when Virginia brought her in, Rosalie looked fairly self-possessed. Poor smiled at her and asked her to sit down. "I'm glad Mrs. Waters explained to you why it's important you should talk to us."

"Yes, sir. She's been very nice," said Rosalie thinly.

"Would you like us to call your mother so she can be here?"

"No!" said Rosalie. "No, please, I—that was part why I wouldn't—Mom—because she'd be mad. I'll—I'll just tell you."

Poor exchanged a look with Virginia, who'd pulled up another chair. "Well, that's fine," he said encouragingly. But Rosalie didn't say anything else for a long minute. He waited.

"Rosalie was afraid her mother'd be angry because she didn't lock the door," said Virginia. "But you just forgot, didn't you?"

Rosalie turned to her gratefully. "That's right. I just forgot —after Mom went out with Ken. I had all this homework to do." She had her light-brown hair tied back today, and it made her look older, but her voice was still thin and childish, belying her warmly rounded little bosom under her blue plaid dress. She took a breath then and told it all at once, as if the sooner she got it out the sooner she could forget it. "It was about seven o'clock when they left, and I just forgot about the door, I had all my homework to do for English and I was working real hard on it because that's my favorite class. And I'd just finished it and wondered what time Mom would be home, but it was too early, it was only ten o'clock, and I went to the kitchen for a Pepsi and when I came back in the living room there was a man there, right inside the door, the door was open, and I remembered I hadn't locked it. And I said who was he and what did he want, and just at first I wasn't scared, but he—he jumped at me and got hold of me and he said— funny things—and he put his hand over my mouth so I couldn't yell and he took me into the bedroom—" She stopped.

Said things. "You remember what he said to you?" asked Poor cautiously.

"I don't know. I don't remember. I was scared, I tried to get away from him—"

"All right," said Poor. "Now just take it easy, Rosalie, and think hard. What did he look like?"

"He wasn't very tall," she said promptly. "About as tall as you, I guess." Five-nine. "He was kind of thin. He had sort of blond hair."

"Do you remember about his clothes?"

"Not much. Oh, and he wasn't very old. I mean, maybe about twenty-five."

Poor felt a little excited. That matched the general description they had, from those first two cases last January, from the neighbor girls on Stephanie Calvert. Medium-sized, fair or sandy, thin, young. "That's very good, Rosalie. Now, can you remember any one thing he said to you? How did he talk—in a regular voice, or loud, or a whisper, or what?"

"He—sort of whispered. I—I don't remember. I was scared, I guess I just didn't hear what he said."

And that could certainly figure. Something else figured too, thought Poor suddenly. "All right. What happened after he hurt you? Why didn't you scream, or—or go to the neighbors?"

Rosalie raised her head and gave him a long grave look; she was blushing slightly. "I—well, I guess I didn't really know—what happened. Just then. I guess I fainted, pretty soon after he got hold of me. And when I came to, I was on the bed and he was gone, and I—well, I guess I thought—just, you know, my monthly thing— And I was afraid Mom'd be mad—about the door, so I just went to bed and when Mom came in I pretended to be asleep. Now I've told you about it, I don't need to tell it over to anybody else, do I?" She turned to Virginia. "I know Mom'll have to know, but you'll tell her, won't you?"

"Sure, honey. Don't worry, she won't be mad."

But Poor was feeling more excited. She'd seen him in the light. "Rosalie—if you saw this man again, would you recognize him? Could you identify him?"

"I don't know," she said hurriedly. "Maybe. Oh, I didn't tell you that—he had a scar on his face. Like from a knife or something."

"On his cheek—forehead—chin?"

"On his cheek, I think it was."

"Right or left side?"

"I don't know. I told you all about it now. I want to go home."

"O.K., Rosalie. Thanks for telling us—you've been a brave girl." He nodded at Virginia, who got up.

"I'll take you home, honey, and stay till your mom gets there."

Poor looked at his scribbled notes, and was making more deductions five minutes later when O'Connor and Varallo came in together.

"But we'd need a goddamned army to check all the hospital records just in L. A. County," O'Connor was saying disgustedly. "So, the probabilities say whoever dumped the bodies knows the area—it could have been from years ago—that goddamned thing could be from a hospital across the country, didn't we say it. I still think the best bet we've got on identifying them is the publicity—but goddamn it, we'll have to cover these names we've turned, just in case."

"Forget the bodies and listen to this," said Poor, and told them about Rosalie. "What do you want to bet? I thought about this and that. For one thing—"

"I'll be damned," said O'Connor, flinging himself down in his desk chair. "That could ring bells, John."

"For one thing, on the first two cases, it looked as if he'd cased the women—to know they lived alone. One apartment, one house. It's very possible he had a look at the place the Calvert girl lives, to pick another woman alone. What I thought was," said Poor, "could it be he was after Mrs. Keating? He might not have known about Rosalie—just seen her mother coming and going. And he came to break in, found the door unlocked, found Rosalie alone there and took her instead. It's roughly the same M.O.—he put her out before he raped her. And she said he whispered. Doesn't remember what, but we can guess."

Varallo sat back and lit a cigarette. "That was Rosalie I saw on the way in, then. Teen-agers. Mmh. They can be touchy as hell. Sensitive—insensitive. And funny things important to them. She was afraid her mother'd be mad about her forgetting the door." He laughed. "A *cavallo donato non si guarda in bocca*."

"Meaning?"

"The old saw about the gift horse."

"But look—she saw him in the light," said Poor. "She gives us a better description than we've had. The scar. The height —age."

"We couldn't depend on her for a legal charge, in a lineup," said O'Connor. "Minors, and you know judges and lawyers. Yeah. But it's something better to go on than what we've had. And"—he sighed gustily, pulled his tie loose and unbuttoned his jacket, and the bulge of the .357 magnum stood out like an extra muscle above his barrel chest—"you know what the hell we do with it, too."

"Don't remind us," said Varallo.

"There are what, fourteen, fifteen men out of our sex records —men with pedigrees of rape—who couldn't show us an alibi on the right time for Calvert. We go back and look at them again—for the scar. And," said O'Connor with a humorless grin, "any of 'em could have acquired the scar since we took a mug shot. We see if they've got alibis for Rosalie. And any of the other ones in our sex records, pedigrees short of rape, could have graduated to rape since last January. Set off by Maggie Walters, for God's sake. And as I've just been thinking on this hospital record thing, we're in the middle of a big metropolitan area. Our boy could be from L.A. or Pasadena or Beverly Hills."

"Let's keep cool," said Poor. "We know he hasn't pulled any rapes, whispering about Maggie, anywhere but Glendale."

"Which doesn't say he lives here, or that he's ever been picked up for anything at all and got into our records. So we look at LAPD's records, for the general description, we look in the sheriff's records—"

"We did that before, on the first two," said Katz behind them. "But that's interesting. I'll go along with John—that's

our boy. Gives us a lot more legwork to do. Damn this thing."
He fingered the bandage irritably. "The doctor said to leave it
on, but it's driving me nuts itching. In this heat."

"Well—end of shift." O'Connor stood up. "Another day tomorrow."

"With all the old and new legwork," said Katz. "Have fun at
it." Tomorrow was his day off.

Varallo drove home in the usual heavy midtown traffic at
that hour; Glendale was getting nearly as bad as Hollywood
or Pasadena. It was still light at this time of day, and as he
came out of the garage he made a detour to check the new
climbers on the trellis outside the patio, Tropicana and Tempo.
There was no sign of aphids; maybe he'd got to them in time.

Laura was setting the table in the dinette. "Vic darling—" she
came to return his kiss, her hands full of silver. "You know,
I'm firmly holding the thought that this one's going to be a
boy and look just like you."

"I detect a subtle note of fulsome flattery," said Varallo.
"You're taking this one a lot easier, aren't you?"

"Oh, well, I got so huge with Ginevra, I wondered if I'd
ever get back to a size fourteen, but I did. I suppose I will this
time. Anyway, I just had another thought, darling." A loud im-
perative feline voice demanded instant admittance, and automatically Varallo leaped to open the back door. Gideon Algernon Cadwallader stalked in, tiger tail erect.

"Yes?" said Varallo suspiciously.

"If it is a boy, what about Cristofero and we call him Cris?"

"For the tenth time, no," said Varallo. "What the hell has
gotten into you? You're not Italian—"

"Merely Scots-Irish. But it'd be silly to call him Patrick or
something—I just think names ought to match," said Laura.
"I think Cris would be cute."

"Cute!" said Varallo. *"Per l'amore de Dio!"*

At eight-forty Traffic fetched a little business in for the night
watch: a trio of juveniles picked up in a brawl outside The Red

Fox Inn on South Brand. Two of them were high on something, not liquor, of course; the other one had had a bag of joints on him and assorted pills—reds, bennies, yellow devils.

"These damn fool kids," said Rhys. They sent the first two to the emergency hospital; one of them passed out just after they were brought in, and it could be an O.D. The third one they'd seen too many of before: the unkempt, dirty, defiant, irresponsible punk, mouthing all the familiar obscenities at the fuzz.

"Goddamned pigs—anybody knows the grass but nothing, man—get it legal pretty soon an' you can't bust nobody for holdin'—"

"And that will be the day," said Rhys. "God forbid." All the research linking the pot with the effects they'd once put down to LSD. But the stupid punks didn't read medical reports.

Dr. Goulding usually took Thursday off. There wasn't anything demanding his immediate attention. He came back to his office on Friday morning to find a new corpse awaiting autopsy, and wondered idly about it as he prepared the body. Good-looking young fellow, didn't look to have been a drunk or derelict.

It wasn't a long or difficult job; he cleaned up, and finished writing the report on it by lunchtime, and sent it up to the detective office. He went out for a leisurely lunch, came back, and was deeply engrossed in an interesting article in the latest issue of The American Hospital Association's house organ, on a vegetarian diet in the treatment of multiple sclerosis, when the daily mail was delivered: one long business-size envelope from the Gray Biological Laboratory. He opened it incuriously.

"Well, I will be damned," he said. "That's funny." He consulted his address book and phoned Norenberg. "The lab report just came in on your Mrs. Fielding. It was an O.D. of Darvon . . . Yes, well, of course we'll have to look into it. Don't dither at me, man, the lab wouldn't make a mistake. I'll have to put in a report, and the detectives will want to talk to you—"

"But that's impossible!" said Norenberg. "That's just ridiculous, Goulding!"

"All I know is what the lab report says," said Goulding testily.

# SIX

Varallo had got out and about on Friday. On the principle of clearing up as they went, he took the names they had from the hospital records to check; and if they were going to go on looking at hospital records, they'd better forget about any of the other routine, he thought. This kind of anonymous thing was always a bastard to work, and it was a tossup as to whether they'd ever get anywhere. You could slog your heart out at it and come up with nothing; or Fate could hand you the answer overnight.

They hadn't done much speculating, about the three little bodies so unceremoniously dumped. A thing like that was beyond speculation, a simple enormity apart from any petty wondering about motive or killer.

They had gone through the indicated motions. Useless to question any householders up there: only two on that new street a mile down from where the bodies had been, and those houses set back from the street. Nobody would remember a car passing, stopping, a month or two back. They knew now, reports coming in as records were sifted, that there were no children reported missing who conformed to the descriptions anywhere in the country. The chances were that the children had belonged together, to the same family; at any rate, they'd been killed and left up there at the same time, so that was likely. But aside from the Wellington kidnap victim back in New Jersey, a year-old boy, there weren't any missing babies NCIC could tell them about, no missing children as young as four and two.

Varallo wasn't pinning any faith to the birth records, though that partial surname was about the best lead they had; it was just a piece of routine to work, and might hand them a jackpot today, six months from now, or not at all.

They had seven names from the first hunt through the birth records. Everybody else was busy at other jobs; he went out to clear away this little piece of routine.

Mrs. Wildman, Idlewood Street . . . It would waste time and invite questions to explain why they were looking at babies; he said something vague about checking hospital records, and people in general were unsuspicious and co-operative. Mrs. Wildman, in fact, had the baby in her arms when she answered the door. Mrs. Aldman, La Crescenta, didn't look old enough to have a baby; the baby visible in a playpen in the front yard. Mrs. Tildman on Myrtle Street, where a clutter of children from five on down sounded noisy enough for fifty kids, around the baby on a blanket in the shade in the side yard. Mrs. Goldman, in a run-down trailer park in Montrose, a slattern, and the baby yelling its head off from the kitchen end of the trailer.

It was a queer little piece of routine, and maybe meant nothing. Varallo landed back at the station at eleven-thirty to find some more routine waiting, but the solid kind you could get your teeth into.

Poor had spent a busy morning: with the better description from Rosalie, he had been back through the records and had pulled a number of files to look at closer. A routine request had been passed on to LAPD yesterday afternoon, and their computers had been busy; they had sent over twenty-four names, complete with Xeroxed rap sheets.

"I just say, we take a long, close look at these four first," said Poor. "In the first place, they all match the description, down to the scar. But also, Vic, their pedigrees with us are short of rape up to last January. All the usual counts that lead up to it—underclothes stolen from lines, exposure, lewd public behavior—"

"Yes," said Varallo. "Crossing T's, with his hangup on Maggie, if he'd committed a rape before that would have got mentioned, and the only rapes we know about are ours. So he could be one with the beginning record, here or somewhere else."

"And with the rapes all in our territory, I say look at these first." Poor handed over the rap sheets and Varallo looked at them, interested, over a cup of coffee from the machine down the hall.

James Daugherty, five counts of indecent exposure, one statutory rape, drunk driving. Twenty-four, Caucasian, five-eight, light brown and blue, a hundred and forty, scar on right cheek, Gregory Silvio, two counts exposure, underclothes theft, disturbing the peace (lewd behavior), twenty-eight, Caucasian, five-nine, a hundred and fifty, brown and brown, scar on upper left jaw. Chester Kidd, exposure, attempted rape, attempted assault, twenty-four, Caucasian, five-eight, a hundred and forty, blond and blue, scar on left cheek. Randall Samuels, one statutory rape, attempted rape, exposure, twenty-nine, Caucasian, five-nine, a hundred and thirty, brown and blue, scar on right cheek. "Suggestive," said Varallo. "Now we know more about his looks, these look good, John."

"I thought so. You've got to go by probabilities—as the boss was saying—and the chances are he's local. Now we know about the scar, we could narrow it down almost to these."

"Let's see if we can find any of these birds to talk to," said Varallo. Everybody else was out somewhere. It was Burt's day off, but he had left a note in his large scrawl on O'Connor's desk.

They had a hasty lunch at the place around the corner and split up to go looking. All four of the men had Glendale addresses. Varallo tried first for Daugherty down on Garfield Avenue, and was told he'd moved; nobody knew where. He tried the nearest post office for a change-of-address and surprisingly got one in Montrose. There, at an old and shabby frame house on a side street, he ran Daugherty to earth: an unhealthy-looking young fellow, sitting in front of an electric fan drinking lukewarm beer out of the can and reading a wrestling magazine. He certainly matched the better description.

"What the hell do cops want now?" he greeted the badge. "I'm clean, I'm off probation, I haven't done anything."

"If you'll answer a few questions, we could finish it right here," said Varallo. "Can you tell me where you were last Tuesday night about ten o'clock?"

"Tuesday—" Daugherty had a slack jaw and a loose mouth; he left his mouth open to think. "Hell, who remembers that far back?"

"What about last Saturday night, early Sunday morning?"

"Now wait a minute. Wait a minute. Tuesday. I was out bowling Tuesday. I don't know what time I got home. This is my sister's place, but her and Bill was out that night, dint get in till after I did. It was that Acme alley down in Glendale, I was alone but the guy there knows me, I'm there a coupla times a week. Damn fuzz, come round bother a guy, get a little outta line once and they never let you forget it." But he didn't ask why Varallo was asking, on what.

At the bowling alley, a fat, incurious proprietor said yeah, he knew Jim Daugherty. "Last Tuesday? Yeah, I guess he was in. I wouldn't say when. All I remember is, he was here when we closed at midnight, he was arguin' with some other guy about how many games they played. He in trouble with the law? Well, count me out—I never said a thing—I don't want to waste time goin' in court."

That wasn't hard and fast, but provisionally it was an alibi. Varallo went looking for Chester Kidd on Jackson Street, and the pretty little gray-haired woman who answered the door said he was at work. "You're a policeman," she said with naïve shrewdness; he hadn't brought out the badge. She'd be familiar with policemen if she knew Chester well. "But he hasn't been doing anything wrong. Lately. Whatever you think. He's been very good, and going to the psychiatrist every week. I see to that —I'm his mother, you know. Chester never means anything bad, he's just weak, poor boy. He never even goes out at night now, and he comes straight home from work. He has a job at a car wash on Colorado."

"He's home every night in the week?" said Varallo genially. "What about last Tuesday?"

"Oh yes," she said quickly, and her eyes flickered. "Every night. With me. Yes, of course he was here Tuesday."

"Thanks so much." Kidd looked a little more interesting, on that, and Varallo went out to the car-wash place and brought him back to the station for questioning.

Kidd was furtive-eyed, sullen, reluctant to talk. "My ma could tell you, I was home all Tuesday night."

"She already has, and we both know what that's worth," said Varallo. "Who's Maggie Walters, Chester?"

"Huh? I never heard of her. I never done anything to her, if she said that. I never."

"What about Tuesday night? Where were you instead of home?"

He looked up just briefly at tall, blond, hard-muscled Varallo looming over him, and looked down again. "Home. I was just home. My ma could say."

It went like that, and after a few futile rounds of it Varallo let him go. Poor came in about then and they compared notes. "I don't know, Vic," said Poor. "Neither Silvio nor Samuels has got an alibi, they're both still on probation. But I didn't get any reaction to Maggie, and wouldn't we, from our boy? None of these punks is very smart."

"No, and why else do we go at it the way we do? You say, we know what you were up to last Tuesday, you were raping Rosalie, and if he is X he says how'd you know—being stupid. Damn it, they all fit that description, they've all got the right records. Keep on hauling them in, pry at them some more." Varallo massaged his jaw. "It'd be a short cut to have the girl take a look at a lineup. If she could or would say. At least we'd be morally sure."

Poor was silent, and then said, "I don't often get a hunch, but I think I'm having one now. He's right here, Vic—right here in Glendale. Somewhere. And this is the routine way to look—the way we have to start to look. He could be one of these four, they all look good for it. But there's always a first time, and maybe he's not in anybody's records. Yet. But I think he's right here."

Varallo knew the feeling, and considering the facts, never mind hunches, he was inclined to agree. But that didn't point any new direction to go looking.

Several things came up all at once on Friday morning, to clutter up the day. Clarence Gantman was due for arraignment, and so was Peter Selby; and the inquest on Reinhart was scheduled for ten o'clock. O'Connor told Wayne he could cover that, told Forbes to cover the arraignments. He called Richard Loomis and by ten o'clock was sitting in the living room of the Loomis house in West Los Angeles asking random questions and getting nowhere.

It was a big, expensive, well-groomed house, and O'Connor, whose education had been improved the last year in regard to furniture prices and mortgage payments, revised his first estimate of Loomis' practice. The elder Mrs. Loomis sat knitting, largely silent, and Loomis' wife seemed more interested in meeting a real-life cop than in the murder; she was thin and nondescript, in too-smart clothes.

"You just caught me—I was going out to make the funeral arrangements. Your office called to say that the—the body could be released. My God, I'm still trying to make sense out of this. Have you found out anything at all?"

"Not much," said O'Connor. "We haven't come across anybody who claims to have talked to your brother later than you did." Wayne had done some of that phoning yesterday.

"My God, do you think we haven't been checking around? Everyone he knew—we knew. There's just nothing. I'll tell you what I'm thinking now—don't know what you'll think of it." Loomis had been pacing the room, and stopped to face O'Connor. "I know you asked me to check if anything was missing, and nothing was. Not that he had much of real value there, jewelry, anything like that. But I'm wondering now if it could have been the—the obvious thing, a burglar, and Barney surprised him and he— The door could have been unlocked, we all forget things occasionally. And the man could have panicked after he hit Barney and just run without ransacking the place."

"Maybe," said O'Connor, noncommittal.

"Well, my God, it's likelier than thinking somebody had a reason to kill him—that's just impossible."

"One thing I'll say, Mr. Loomis. Sometimes emotions get triggered off by very little. You tell us your brother seldom lost his temper, but somebody could have built up a grudge on him out of nothing at all. It happens. Have you been able to think of any little disagreement, any trouble he had with anybody, over anything at all—that he might have mentioned to you?"

The younger Mrs. Loomis said brightly, "Well, there was that client. If that's the kind of thing you mean, Lieutenant."

"Oh, don't be silly, Lois. That couldn't possibly be anything to—"

"What client?" asked O'Connor.

"Last April. He raised a fuss, said Barney hadn't done his taxes right. His name was Hunnicutt, such a ridiculous name."

"That's ridiculous," said Loomis.

"Well, you never know," said O'Connor.

The elder Mrs. Loomis put down her knitting. "The only time I ever remember Barney losing his temper was in junior high school when another boy called him a sissy for liking to play chess. You remember, Rich? He knocked him down and gave him a bloody nose. The boy didn't know Barney was interested in boxing too." She smiled.

"Was he?" asked O'Connor.

"Oh—at one time," said Loomis. "He was rather—well, a bit of a fanatic on physical fitness. He always tried to keep in condition—the regular diet, and exercise, and all that. He'd just quit smoking, not that he ever smoked more than four or five a day—he'd been after me to quit."

Which made it a little unlikelier that a surprised burglar could have taken him, thought O'Connor. He felt, irrationally, a little irritated at the model young man B. J. Loomis. He went on talking to them, listening, but nothing more emerged. Nothing unusual had showed up in the bank records.

However, as he knew for his sins—as any experienced cop knew—very small things could set off homicides. Or assaults, or whatever. In its wisdom the law did not require motive to be shown in homicide, because motive could be quite irrelevant. One man might utter a swear-word over what would set another man committing violence; there was just no way to guess at possible motives.

O'Connor automatically got on the right freeway and drove back to Glendale, found a slot on the street, and walked half a block to the C. P. Adrian Tax Agency. As he came in, all three of the stenos at work in the front section fastened interested eyes on him; the other one, the redheaded one, was at the back in the cubicle belonging to Jim Dumbarton. The little clatter and conversation in the room seemed to stop for a moment as they registered the presence of a cop.

One of the girls got up, a sheaf of papers in her hand to make excuse, and came around the wooden gate that shut off the typists' section. "Oh, can I help you? You're the police officer who was here—Lieutenant O'Connor."

"That's right, Miss Mederos."

"Do you want anything? Have you found out yet how Mr. Loomis was killed? We're all pretty interested, you know." She smiled at him.

But now that O'Connor had learned more about that stuffed shirt, the priggish B. J. Loomis, he wasn't much interested in his former colleagues. None of them had liked him or disliked him much: the damned fellow was so colorless, so correct, nobody could have felt much about him. It was quite natural that nobody had been interested enough to check on him when he didn't show for work. "I just want to have another look at his desk," said O'Connor, and brushed past the girl.

The various accounts Loomis had worked on were so neatly arranged that he put his hand on the one he was after in three minutes. Christian W. Hunnicutt III, it was labeled, and O'Connor opened it on Loomis' desk and looked it over without bothering to sit down. The pompously named Hunnicutt was, it appeared, a writer: TV and films. O'Connor glanced at the tidy notations, lists of figures, and his eyebrows shot up. Program names familiar to him, studios: Mr. Hunnicutt was dragging down a very respectable hunk of yearly money, probably for very little work. There was an address in La Cañada.

Every eye in the place followed him out.

And for all he knew Hunnicutt was in some studio in Beverly Hills or Hollywood, or did writers keep regular working hours, or write TV scripts at home? He wouldn't know.

It was a fourth-floor apartment in a big new modern building on a superior winding street in that very upper-class section of town. For a bachelor (which had appeared on the tax forms) he did himself well: about four hundred a month, O'Connor reckoned. And he was there. Whether he'd been writing or not O'Connor couldn't tell; there wasn't a book or a desk in the violently futuristic room he stepped into. Faintly lascivious murals on two walls, a grass-green carpet, barrel-shaped yellow chairs, glass tables, and a large, white-leather-padded bar in one corner were the salient features of the place. There was also one wall of glass, and the noon sun glared through, not quite overhead what with the damned double daylight saving; but the air conditioning must have been turned down to sixty.

"A lieutenant of *police?* Goodness gracious, what have I been up to?" wondered Hunnicutt.

O'Connor looked at him sourly. But of course you never did know—people came all shapes and sizes, and at least Hunnicutt wasn't impossible for it, not a small or frail man. He was tall and willowy, about forty, a poem in blended soft greens, slacks, sports shirt and scarf loose at his throat; he had a high-bridged nose and a soft voice.

"Oh," he said when O'Connor asked a few questions. "Oh,

that. What a bore all this business is, but one does like to keep all one can, you know. All the tiresome taxes. Well, it was the first time this firm had done them for me, and one had to be sure they—the fellow who was actually making up the forms—understood all the, ah, ramifications of my silly job. All the deductions I'm allowed, you know. One doesn't like to overlook anything—library fines, for instance, I'm always forgetting to take books back—. But why on earth are the police interested?"

"Were you satisfied with the job Loomis did in the end?"

"I'd really forgotten his name, if I ever heard it. Oh, I suppose so. They were recommended to me by somebody or other, I really forget, but there, I'm so vague. Don't tell me the police are interested in them? They've been falsifying—" Hunnicutt looked momentarily terrified.

"Not that we know of." O'Connor cast another glance around the incredible place, thanked him, and thankfully went out.

It was Burt's day off, but he had left a note on O'Connor's desk. "So far only L.'s prints on anything from apt., except bookend. Four dandy latents on, not in ours, sent LAPD and DC." O'Connor felt slightly better, reading that; in the end, the physical evidence usually provided answers. Varallo had left him a note too: all the babies turned up yesterday on those surnames were present and accounted for. O'Connor scowled at that; the very anonymous one, those bodies, and they might never know any more than they did now.

He realized suddenly that what with all the driving around it was nearly one o'clock and he was starving. He went out to lunch, wondering where everybody was. At least nothing new had gone down.

When he came in again, Duff hailed him from the desk. "That J.D. just got bailed—the one they picked up for holding last night. The parents came in, cussing out the fuzz. Just innocent childish pranks, and we keep picking on the kids."

"Now, Al—I've just had lunch."

This time there was something new on his desk: the autopsy report on Loomis. He read it rapidly, scanning it over for the one point he was interested in. General condition of body excellent, and so on and so on—one hard blow to left temple, bone fractured, death practically instantaneous: no other marks on body—subject had eaten a meal approximately three hours prior to death, consisting of vegetable protein, carrots, green beans, milk, gelatin— "Him and his health food," muttered O'Connor. Estimated time of death, between 7 P.M. Friday and 7 P.M. Saturday last.

O'Connor growled over that and got Goulding on the phone. "Can't you pin this down any closer?"

"Not after all that time, damn it. I talked to Forbes about it—he said the air conditioning was on, too. That would affect the decaying process. That's all I can tell you, in round terms."

"Friday or Saturday. Well, are you sure he was dead by Saturday midnight, say?"

"I think you can be reasonably sure about that, yes. Burt sent that glass bookend down. I can't say positively, but it's the kind of thing could very well account for that blow."

"Thanks for nothing."

"Have you got a line on those bodies yet?"

"I don't know. We hope so." But, it suddenly struck O'Connor, it shouldn't be so anonymous, that thing. Children. Adults could walk away and not get missed—how many did, every year?—but children were supervised, counted, noticed. Usually, he amended to that: these children had been neglected children. Still—

He was still sitting there, ruminating on the children, on B. J. Loomis, when Varallo and Poor came in, and they kicked the rapist around some.

"I can see your four locals for it just dandy," said O'Connor, "matching the description, that scar—but you'd think, with that type, we'd get a reaction to Maggie. If one of them is him. And we checked out everybody in our sex files before, for any connection to a Maggie Walters. N.G. I might buy your hunch, John, that he's not in anybody's files yet. Right here, but not showing for what he is."

"Is it any use to have Rosalie look at these four? It could be a quick way to know. If she points one out, lean on him and he'd probably come apart," said Varallo.

"Yeah. Yeah," said O'Connor slowly. "I think we do that, Vic."

Wayne came in looking pleased with himself and said he'd caught up to the burglars on that furniture-store job. "Just a question of working through records. I came up with one of 'em about the twentieth name in, and he told me who his pal was. They'd kept part of the loot. I just booked them in."

"Congratulations," said O'Connor absently, and the phone light flashed on. "O'Connor . . . What? Oh, for God's sake, Goulding . . . Well, I see it, I see it, but— What? He glanced at his watch. "Little of the working day left. All right, we'll expect you. Of all the damned things," he added, putting the phone down. "Goulding's just handed us another homicide. Oh, nothing big—without much doubt a suicide. But something to work on some, do the paperwork, damn it."

Varallo put out his cigarette and stood up. "I'd better see about that lineup. Tomorrow. How do we do it, Charles? Chance she'd be confused if we lined all four up with a mixed bag of other citizens. Stand them up one at a time? But we could come to some conclusion—know definitely, if she does pick one."

"I'll have to call Mrs. Keating," said Poor. "She'll probably want to come too."

"I tell you, it's impossible," said Dr. Norenberg.

"Well, it happened." Goulding had just brought him into the office, handed the lab report to O'Connor.

"I'm not saying it's impossible she committed suicide." Norenberg was distressed; his one characteristic, that overconscientiousness, was transparent in his whole attitude. "Damn it,

I liked the woman. I've been their family physician for twenty
years—they're nice people. I was damned sorry for her—Mrs.
Fielding—but these things happen. You do what you can, and
when you can't do any more—" he shrugged. "I hope some day
we'll find a cure for rheumatoid arthritis. That's all that was
wrong with her, if you want to say all. She was getting progressively more helpless, of course. She'd been at home till
about two years ago—there's a husband and daughter, both
quite devoted to her—but it got to be too much care for them.
Mr. Fielding's past eighty, has some emphysema, he can't do
much lifting, and the daughter couldn't be on duty twenty-
four hours a day. She's not married, works here in town. Mrs.
Fielding had been in this convalescent home the last two
years, and it's an excellent place—very efficiently run. There's
not a chance she could have got hold of that overdose there.
The medication is all supervised very strictly."

"She could have saved it up," said Goulding. "What was she
getting of the Darvon, three a day, four?"

"Four if needed, and aspirin, and a sleeping capsule if she
asked for it. I'd doubt that. The people at those places are
trained to watch for that, among other things."

"But she was depressed. About the pain, and so on."

"Well, yes poor woman. She was an intelligent woman—
her mind wasn't affected at all, of course—and she knew she'd
just get progressively worse, more pain, and that it might be
years," said Norenberg. "She'd said it to me often enough, why
did she have to drag on like this, no use to anybody, and she
wished the Lord would take her. But she never struck me as the
type—still, I do see it's the only answer. But—convalescent
homes as good as that don't make mistakes, and anyway a mistake like that is just inconceivable."

"You'd think so," said O'Connor dryly. "Estimated amount
equal to thirty-five Darvon capsules. I've seen an O.D. on
twenty. What about the family, Dr. Norenberg?"

"Oh no, no," said Norenberg fussily. "They were devoted—
quite devoted. Fielding's a very nice fellow. The daughter's a

nice woman. In any case, to come down to hard facts—which is what you want to hear, I suppose—if you're thinking either the husband or daughter could have slipped it to her out of pity—but I don't suppose for a moment either of them would do such a thing—they couldn't have. When Mrs. Fielding went into the convalescent home all her medication went with her—I checked it at the time. Ever since then the Darvon prescription has been supplied by the convalescent home. Mr. Fielding has a prescription for nitroglycerin—and the daughter is on Aldomet for high blood pressure, but that doesn't enter in."

"What's the money situation?" asked O'Connor.

"Oh, I should think quite substantial," said Norenberg. "He's a retired realtor, had his own agency here. They live up on Mountain. My bills have always been paid promptly, no question, and there was no difficulty about the convalescent home."

"Well, so that takes care of that," said Varallo. "That's a little teaser, Charles—how did she get hold of it?"

"Which is all you have to find out," said Goulding. "Personally I don't blame the poor soul. Nothing to look forward to but more pain and eventual helplessness, and her mind still functioning. Hell of a thing. And those places are damned depressing, even the best of them. A lot of old people waiting around to die, half of 'em without any minds left—my God, I know those places, from when I was in private practice. I don't know how they get anybody to work in them. Enough to make anybody want to commit suicide."

Poor spoke up unexpectedly; he'd been sitting smoking quietly, listening. "I know. Ann's grandmother was in one of those homes for a couple of years, we used to go see her sometimes. I'll tell you what occurs to me. The people they do get to work in those homes—a lot of them, I mean—are the types who're sympathetic, really like the old people. Oh, the ones to do the cleaning up, cooking, just hired help. But the attendants I saw at this place, nurses' aides and practical nurses, were mostly—nice. Kind. I suppose it could be that one like that felt so sorry for this woman, if she begged—"

"Quite impossible." This time it was Norenberg and Goulding together. "Don't mistake sympathetic professional care for sentimentality, John," said Goulding cynically. "That's not possible on a couple of counts. There wouldn't be many R.N.'s there, but some. It's required by law that an R.N. supervise all prescriptive medication, and it'll be kept locked up, doled out as prescribed by the doctor. By an R.N. And there are nurses and nurses, but I've yet to meet one who'd forget all her training to be that sympathetic."

"Besides, we could check the supply," said Norenberg. "In fact we will. An enormous amount like that—it couldn't just disappear and not be noticed. It'd have been spotted right away, by the R.N. in charge. There's an R.N. on duty in every wing of that place round the clock."

"Little mystery," said Varallo, intrigued.

"Oh hell," said O'Connor. "There's nothing in it—we know it must have been suicide. I see we've got to try to pin it down, but with everything else— Damnation, Norenberg, why didn't you take it as an act of God and let it go? She was seventy-nine."

"I'm just as glad I didn't, Lieutenant. One thing we do know, she had to have help in getting hold of it. She couldn't get out of bed without help—she couldn't walk. And if there's somebody in that place, or coming into that place, with access to drugs, who's willing to hand them out, we ought to find out who it is."

"Well, I wash my hands of the whole business," said Goulding vigorously. "If I ever land in one of those hellholes, with or without my mind, I hope to God some good samaritan comes along to hand me the lethal dose. Oh, I see what you mean—we can't have people running around handing out prescriptive drugs for the asking. But however it happened, at least the poor woman's out of her misery." He stood up. "If you ever find out, let me know. I'm more concerned about those kids."

"So am I," said O'Connor. And, of course, with Loomis; but they had some physical evidence on Loomis, for whatever it turned out to be worth. The rapist—that was something else. There had been follow-up stories in all the papers about the children; those still could bring in someone who knew something.

It was Rhys's night off, and Hunter was holding down the night watch alone. Friday nights were usually quiet, people getting ready for the weekend.

He listened in to the Traffic calls awhile, bored sitting there alone; he was almost relieved when he got a call from the desk at nine o'clock.

"Heist at a liquor store," said Harrison, sounding bored too. "Kenneth and Grandview."

Hunter drove up there, thinking about O'Connor spotting that heister just on the description the other day; well, O'Connor had been on this force thirteen years, and he was quite a guy. Up on Kenneth, the black-and-white was still there, Stoner inside the store, Chris and Tom's.

"Listen," the man behind the counter was saying to Stoner, "I hope I've got some sense, Officer." He was a big man with a lot of curly gray hair. "I've been in this business for fifteen years, and it isn't the first time I got held up. The wild ones around lately—or not so lately. Who're you?—oh, more cops," as Hunter came up. "Detective, hah? Pleased to meet you. I was just saying, it's not the first time I got held up, and way things are, I intend to stay in business, and I took some time off last year, took that course the NRA gives in shooting for self-protection. I keep the gun right here, see." He reached under the counter and produced it professionally, a nearly new Police Positive .38. "And if some hood had walked in here and showed the gun and said hand over, I tell you, boys, I'd have fetched this out and let him have it." He said it regretfully, looking at the gun.

"But you didn't? Why not?" asked Hunter.

"Well, I hope I've got some common sense. They came in, ordinary customers—you can see I carry a lot of things besides the liquor—the freezer goods, dairy goods, canned stuff, the gourmet section there—and I'm sitting here looking at the *National Enquirer* till they're ready to bring the merchandise up and pay. And when all of a sudden they come up to the counter and one of them says, this is a heist, mister, and I see the gun— Am I crazy? I ask you? A dame with a gun, who knows what she's going to do? Waving it around—who takes chances like that? I opened the register like a good little boy and handed over. Brother—a dame! I should've said, two dames."

"Oh-oh," said Hunter. "One about medium height, brown hair, the other one blond and taller?"

"Yeah, that's right. You know them? They're pros? I'll be damned. But I haven't told you the damndest thing. The blonde had a baby with her—cute little baby, in one of those backpack things."

"What about the gun?" asked Hunter resignedly. There hadn't been any lead on the female heisters at all, and probably wouldn't be. "Did you see a car, when they left—notice anything else?"

"No, sorry. Out they went—they were the only ones in, now I think they hung around till one other customer left. And there are a lot of cars around, everything here open tonight." There were seven or eight stores along here, and the drugstore across the street. "The gun I can say about. It was an automatic, about the size of a .32. An automatic yet—all I can say is, I'm not about to commit suicide, if you see what I mean."

Hunter saw. And this didn't give them anything more except the gun, which was no lead at all. This time they'd collected about three hundred bucks.

Stoner went back on tour and Hunter went back to the office to write the report. He figured the lieutenant wouldn't like the report at all; the lieutenant liked to see cases get solved and X's booked in. But when they didn't have one damned thing to work with, there just wasn't anywhere to go.

O'Connor didn't like Hunter's report one damned bit. These two females going around taking the loot, the amateurs, and nowhere to go on it.

"And damn the descriptions, nowhere to go on the rapist, if Rosalie doesn't pick out one of those four definitely."

"You're not usually so pessimistic, Charles." Varallo put down Hunter's report and lit a cigarette. "The lineups are set for some-time this afternoon. John'll fetch Rosalie in. Do we go look at more hospital records?"

"Hell, what we turned up, looking locally—use up a lot of time for damn all." O'Connor ran a hand through his curly black hair. "I'm putting more faith in the stories in the papers— hell, somebody must have noticed, when three kids just van-ished? Two kids and a baby? On Loomis, wait for the kickback from the Feds on those prints. The solid physical evidence. Maybe we'll find out who, and why afterward."

"Fingerprints," said Varallo, "are useful only if they're on file somewhere."

"And, damn it," said O'Connor, "I suppose we've got to do some work on this suicide. Nothing in it, but it's another funny little thing."

"Which intrigues me," said Varallo. "I'll look at it." Forbes, Katz, and Poor were all in; Poor was brooding over those sex pedigrees, talking to Katz. Wayne came in briskly, and the light flashed on O'Connor's phone. He picked it up.

"You've got a new burglary," said Duff, "and the citizen's mad."

"Naturally," said O'Connor.

"No, he's mad at us. He says he did just what the police told him to do, protect his property, and it didn't do any good at all. He wants to talk to Tracy, and it's Tracy's day off."

"For God's sake," said O'Connor, "why Tracy?"

"I don't know. It's Burchett Street," said Duff.

"Idle hands," said O'Connor, annoyed. "My God."

# SEVEN

The citizen's name was Ronald Elworthy, and he was right-
eously angry. He said to Varallo, "Don't we all know the crime
rate is up, and I thought I'd done what I could in the way of pre-
cautions. You'll want a list of what's gone—I've been trying to
check. My wife—my God, I hate to call and tell her, she'll be
wild—I don't think we've spent a night away from home in five
years, but her mother's been sick and we stayed over there last
night, Marge is still there—and I come home and find this
mess! The TV, the portable radio, my tape recorder, all Marge's
jewelry, her fur coat—"

"If you'll just show me where he got in," said Varallo.

"The back door. That's the other thing, damn it." This was
an old English brick place on an older residential street, a
house solidly built. Elworthy led him through a gloomy dining
room to the kitchen and service porch. "I'm *aware* of the rise in
crime, Officer—worried about it. I went to this talk at the library, sponsored by your department. What Citizens Can Do to
Prevent Crime. It was one of your officers, a man named Tracy,
and—"

"Oh yes," said Varallo. The door leading out of the service
porch was a Hollywood door, glass panel above the knob. Most
police forces were sponsoring those informal meetings with citizens; Patrolman Tracy was one of several Glendale men deliv-
ering the little lectures around. "Did you touch this door, sir?
You found it just like this?"

"That's right, I remembered that too," said Elworthy. "If you
are the victim of a crime, don't touch anything until the police
have examined it. This Tracy said, about these signs. About

marking things for identification, with that special tool to mark anything—you can rent it from the police."

"That's right," said Varallo. The burglar had had no trouble getting in; it was a neat enough pro job. He had used a glass cutter on the lower pane in the door, lifted it out, reached through and unlocked the door by the little button in the knob. "Did you?"

"I hadn't got around to it yet, but Tracy said these signs—like that," said Elworthy, "ALL VALUABLES MARKED FOR IDENTIFICATION, were very often a deterrent just by themselves. Even when things hadn't been, a burglar coming to break in and seeing it wouldn't take the chance, just go on somewhere else."

"That's been our general experience," said Varallo. He had brought along a lab kit, and was carefully dusting the lifted-out pane of glass.

"General experience!" said Elworthy. "Hah! I got three of those signs made up specially, for all the doors, you can see for yourself, and a lot of damn good it was! Leave the place all locked up tight and go away for half a day, and come back to find this! Marge kept saying we ought to get a solid door there—"

"Well, you know, Mr. Elworthy," said Varallo, "it'd be simpler to have a double lock put on this door. Without that, it's a very easy door to get in, even if it's locked."

"Double lock?"

"Yes, sir. It's an extra Yale lock installed above the knob, so that you have to have a key. With that, even if the glass is out, nobody can reach in and unlock the door, the way he did here."

"Oh, I didn't know about that. But this officer said these signs are one of the best protections, and the hell of a lot of use they are, you ask me!"

Varallo sympathized, took a list of what was missing. He had brought out a few clear latents on the glass, and Elworthy said his wife had washed all the kitchen windows yesterday and, no, he hadn't touched that, so Varallo didn't ask for his prints to compare. He went back to the station and handed the lifted prints over to Burt. But the Hollywood door had started a train of thought in his mind.

"Loomis' apartment," he said. "The Traffic men broke in— the door was locked. A double lock, somebody said. Was it locked all the way?"

"What made you think about that?" asked Burt. "As a matter of fact, no. I had a look to be sure. The regular lock was on, the spring lock in the knob, but the extra one wasn't locked. Why?"

But it wouldn't have been, of course. Loomis would have had to lock it with a key from inside, and he'd been dead. "Just curious," said Varallo. A dim picture rose in his mind. Fairly early in the evening then—Friday or Saturday—because Loomis hadn't yet locked the door? Or somebody coming, and Loomis unlocking the extra lock to let whoever in. Somebody getting mad at Loomis, hitting out with the snatched-up bookend, and running out, the door slamming behind.

Meanwhile, there was the little mystery of Mrs. Fielding's Darvon. The report on the burglary could wait. Poor and O'Connor were busy setting up the lineups for this afternoon; where Katz and Forbes had got to he didn't know. He drove down to West Broadway and found the Broad Heights Convalescent Home.

He realized, parking and walking back, that he'd never been in one of these places. His own parents had died, one after the other, of short illnesses in the hospital. Laura's father had died of a heart attack at forty, her mother in that hit-run accident. Remembering what Goulding had said, he went into the lobby with some curiosity.

It looked like a nice, clean place, linoleum floor shining with wax, a couple of innocuous pictures on the walls, a couch, occasional chairs: a door labeled RECEPTIONIST, closed. Three elderly people in wheelchairs were the sole occupants of the lobby. One old man, shaking constantly with a palsy, his eyes vacant on the front door; one old woman, head thrown back so that she stared at the ceiling: one hand reached out in a constant, meaningless gesture. The second old lady was knitting, and her smile was kind.

"Hello there, young man. You'll find Mrs. Corbett in the front office if you're looking for her."

Varallo thanked her and tried the RECEPTIONIST door; it was open, and he went in and showed the badge to the woman at the desk.

"We've been expecting you. Dr. Norenberg called, and I must say we've been upset about that. We've never had such a thing happen here, and just how it did happen we don't know, except that I can assure you, wherever Mrs. Fielding got the Darvon, it wasn't out of our stock." She was all business, a middle-aged woman with a good figure in a white pantsuit, wearing an R.N.'s cap. "I'm Mrs. Corbett—what? Oh no, the receptionist is Miss Rafferty, she's not here on Saturdays but she couldn't help you much on this anyway. Since Dr. Norenberg called, we've been trying to reach some conclusion—I've been talking to everybody in that wing—and we're running a check on all the Darvon. Of course a number of our patients get that. But it's quite impossible that Mrs. Fielding could have got hold of any here."

"That's what Norenberg said. How can you be so sure?"

"Well, he's right." She gave him a warm smile. "I didn't know we had such good-looking detectives, Mr. Varallo—you'll forgive my saying that, I must be old enough to be your mother. We all liked Mrs. Fielding, you know—she was a nice old lady. In a place like this, as maybe you wouldn't know, so many of our patients are mentally afflicted, or childish, it's always a pleasure to have one like Mrs. Fielding, so alert mentally. Of course her physical condition was deteriorating. You do understand that she couldn't walk, couldn't get out of bed without assistance?"

"We went over it with the doctor. Did she have many visitors?"

"Oh yes. Somebody was in to see her every day. The family came every day, of course. But we don't keep tabs on visitors, of course. I want to show you just how everything is done, so you can see for yourself what—er—tight security we run," and she gave him another smile.

Varallo followed her up a long corridor. Double doors to the left led into a large, well-furnished lounge—couches, chairs, a color TV, tables, a bookcase. The TV was on to a talk show. Perhaps a dozen people were in there, most of them in wheelchairs. Nearest the door sat a thin, nearly bald old woman firmly tied into a wheelchair with a length of sheeting. A hospital gown was rucked up around her neck, she had one leg drawn up contortedly and was patting her bony knee, mumbling to herself. Down the corridor, past doors to a stainless steel kitchen, were ranged other wheelchairs. An old, old man bundled up in a sweater, who cackled at Varallo and stretched out a hand. An old, old woman who had pulled her hospital gown half off and peered at them slyly. Mrs. Corbett stopped there and said, "Now, Julia. You promised you'd be good today," adjusted the gown and retied the linen straps round the chair.

And Varallo could see what Goulding had been talking about. The old people, with or without families, living beyond the life of their faculties: marking time here waiting to die, needing the constant care. He supposed a good number of them would be on Medicare; it would probably cost a bit to keep a patient here, the nice clean place, the efficient, kind help.

Where another corridor crossed, Mrs. Corbett stopped. "This is the nurses' station for this wing. Oh, Geraldine, this is the police officer, Mr. Varallo. Mrs. Potter. I want to show him just how everything's done. First of all, the drugs." Mrs. Potter wore an R.N.'s cap too, but all up the corridors they had passed other white-clad attendants, both sexes: practical nurses, aides.

Mrs. Potter said in a troubled voice, "We've been over it and over it, since Dr. Norenberg called. None of us can understand how it happened."

"Well now, look." Mrs. Corbett took out a bunch of keys. Beside the long counter, with its telephone, rank of lights above, intercom, was a cumbersome metal cabinet looking like an overgrown safe. "There are twenty-eight patients in this wing, Mr. Varallo, and twelve of them have been prescribed various drugs by their doctors. That is, prescriptive painkillers and so on, drugs which could be harmful in quantity, you understand. Like Mrs. Fielding's Darvon—some of those patients get Darvon too." She selected a key, fitted it into the lock, and the entire front of the cabinet swung open to show a dozen slide-out trays. "You see the arrangement." She slid out the top tray; it contained a row of plastic medicine bottles, all labeled; Varallo picked one up. MR. SALTER, EMPIRIN NO. 4, ONE EVERY 6 HRS. DR. KING. "Only the R.N.'s have keys to these, you see. And everything is in the book—" She indicated that, a big, ledgerlike thing open on the desk. "Which patient gets what, when, and when each patient last had medication—so the different aides coming in as the shifts change have an exact record. For instance, if a patient asks for a pain pill, the aide would check the book to be sure when the last one was given, and ask the R.N. on duty. She'd have to get the R.N. to get the medication. And as you can see, all the medication is kept under the patient's individual name."

"Yes, I see."

"We deal with a big pharmacy in Alhambra, all the prescriptions go directly there as the doctors hand them to us. Now suppose I show you Mrs. Fielding's room. The new patient isn't in yet?"

"Not till this afternoon," said Mrs. Potter. "The husband asked us to arrange for an ambulance."

"I've never known a bed to stay vacant that long," commented Mrs. Corbett, leading him up the corridor. "As a rule there's a waiting list." Too many of the old, old people, thought Varallo, and worn-out families desperate for help in looking after them. He rather felt the way Goulding did: the lethal dose preferable. He had glimpses into the rooms as they passed. Four-bed rooms to the left, two-bed rooms to the right; there were wide windows looking into pleasant shaded patios, and all the rooms looked clean, if rather bare and not very big; in two of them portable TV's were on. Along this corridor a fat old lady was slowly pushing a metal walker. There were more wheelchairs, with vacant-eyed old people in them. In one room they passed a fretful voice was calling monotonously, "Nurse—nurse —nurse!"

"This was Mrs. Fielding's room." Mrs. Corbett stood back to let him in. "And this is Miss Dilbeck. She shared the room with Mrs. Fielding all the while she was with us."

Varallo looked around. It was a room about fifteen feet square, the far side of it all glass, a sliding door onto a wide central patio with trees, shrubs. There were two hospital beds, with tracks above for curtains to pull around each; a small bedside chest beside each bed. In the side wall was a door open on a minute lavatory, a built-in washbasin, and two very narrow doors right together. Mrs. Corbett swung one of those open to reveal a closet about two feet wide, a narrow shelf above. There certainly wasn't much room for concealment of anything, Varallo decided: or apparently much privacy. All the room doors had been open, nurses and attendants all over the place.

"She's dead, isn't she, and she was younger than me!" said the other woman in the room.

"Now, Dorothy—"

Varallo swung round to look at the old woman in the wheelchair inside the door. She was regarding him with very bright little dark eyes; she looked hardly bigger than a child, shrunken with age, but her cracked voice was shrill and strong. "She wanted to die, Bertha did, but I don't. Not so long as I've got my appetite and an eye for a handsome man." She giggled.

"Dorothy!" said Mrs. Corbett. "Now behave yourself. Have you seen all you want, Mr. Varallo? If you'd like to come back to the office, I'll show you how the orders are made up for the pharmacy, and how they're distributed as they're delivered. We keep an individual check on everything, we have to."

"She wanted to die, but she said 'twas a sin to interfere with the Lord's plan. But she died and I'm still alive!" Miss Dilbeck announced triumphantly.

Varallo followed the subdued click of Mrs. Corbett's heels back down the hall, and like a refrain that ran through his mind all the way. *She said 'twas a sin to interfere with the Lord's plan* . . .

"Dr. Norenberg called us," said Rupert Fielding. "I—we supposed someone would come from the police." He stepped back. "You'd better come in. Oh, this is my daughter Louise."

Varallo followed him from the old-fashioned tiled entry hall to a big sunken living room, shadowy and barnlike. This was an old house, and a huge oleander outside all but obscured the front windows of the room. "Please sit down. We've been talking it over, but I'm afraid we're just at a loss as to what happened."

"Well, Mr. Fielding, it looks as if your wife managed somehow to get hold of an overdose. We're just trying to find out how, because obviously she must have had help."

"We'd better have a light." The woman switched on one small table lamp.

"I just don't know," said Fielding. He was a big man, but stooped somewhat with age; he had been a fine-looking man, strong regular features, still plentiful white hair, but his skin was mottled with brown spots and he had a bad color, gray and drawn. He sat on the edge of a chair, hands shaking slightly between his knees, and shook his head. "I don't know. I just don't know."

"It's just made it all the worse, wondering," said his daughter. She looked like him: a tall woman, slightly mannish, not pretty, in the fifties, looking rather shabby in a plain black dress. "I never thought Mama'd have done such a thing, and we just can't make out how it happened. We were surprised when the doctor asked for an autopsy, but it seems now he suspected something. Well, Dr. Norenberg wouldn't make a mistake. But it's just made it all the worse."

They looked at Varallo helplessly. After a long moment Fielding said, "It seems so strange, all this week. Not to have her there any longer. Nowhere to go, nothing to plan. I never thought how that would be—of course we always thought I should go first. We were married fifty-five years. It's a long time."

"Yes, sir, it is." Varallo felt a little helpless too. It was quite impossible to ask them, did she beg you to help her, did you somehow smuggle the Darvon in?

"And since she'd been down there, it made a pattern to the day—do you know what I mean? I'd generally get there at lunchtime, to help her with that, and stay all the afternoon. Until Louise came. I'd go down on the bus. I gave up driving last year, the doctor felt— And now there's nothing to do. Nothing to do for her any more."

"Papa. At least we know she's at rest, and out of pain. I work at Robinson's, I used to be at the downtown store but when they built the one here I asked for a transfer, it's so much more convenient. I'd meet Papa down at the home, and we'd see she had her dinner, and then come on home. It does—feel queer, her not there any more. After all that time."

Varallo thought absently, as he assessed these two, the mother unable to look after the house physically, maybe for some years; the daughter too occupied with her job, with caring for the mother before she went into the home. It was an old house, once a good house, and big, on this once fashionable street north in the city. But this big room looked bare, the shabby rug was too small for the floor space, and while everything seemed clean enough, it wore a general look of decay and gloom.

"Mrs. Corbett—at the convalescent home—said your mother had a good many friends come to see her. Could you tell me their names?"

"Why, yes. But you can't think any of them would have— have got the medicine for her. Even if they could have. It'd be wicked, they wouldn't." Louise Fielding looked shocked. "I know it's queer, how you feel about things. One way, I'm so glad for her she hasn't any more pain and misery, and another, it just doesn't seem possible she's gone. Like—a candle gone out, all of a sudden. And I know she said—she wanted to go—but she knew it'd be wrong—oh, I'm sorry. You asked about people coming. Well, there's Mrs. Ochsman, they were old friends, they went to school together. And Mrs. Wooley and Miss Pridhoff from the church—a lot of the church people went to see her when they could. But I just don't understand how it could have happened! It couldn't possibly have been a mistake—down there—because it's such a good place, they were all so kind to her, you know that, Papa."

"A very nice place," said Fielding slowly. "Yes. She liked it—at first. She tried to keep cheerful, not to complain. But it was depressing. All those old people—" and he laughed suddenly. "Life is a very strange thing, isn't it? I forget I'm old too. Bertha was old. Fifty-five years. And now there's nothing I can do for her any more."

"Papa—"

Somewhere in another room a telephone rang, and Louise Fielding excused herself. She came back in a few moments and said, "It was about the ad. Someone who wants to buy the wheelchair."

"That's good," he said absently.

"If you could give me some addresses, Miss Fielding," said Varallo.

"Oh yes. But that's silly, thinking any of them would have done such a thing. Friends."

As Varallo got out his notebook, for no reason he was thinking again about Dorothy Dilbeck: *she's dead and I'm still alive . . .*

Katharine and Laura went out on Saturday morning to look at the interesting old cradle Katharine had spotted in an antique shop out on Eagle Rock Boulevard. "But they'll probably want seventeen prices for it," she hissed at Laura as they went in. "There wasn't any price tag."

"There never is in these places, they ask what they think the traffic will bear. Wrinkle your nose at it and say it might do if it was refinished," advised Laura, and immediately spoiled it by adding, "But it's perfectly adorable, Katharine! With a good polish, and one of those cute colonial patchwork quilts, it'd be perfect—you've got mostly maple in the nursery anyway—"

"May I help you, ladies?"

"Well, I was rather interested in this, it might do," said Katharine vaguely. "How much is it?"

"I can let you have it for seventy-five."

Laura laughed lightly. "Of course you know that's outrageous. It's not an *antique*. Everything new's so expensive, my friend thought she might find something just to do, secondhand —of course it isn't everyone would want an old thing like that, but we'd take it off your hands for any reasonable price, say thirty dollars."

"Seventy-five, ma'am."

"Well, after all," said Katharine half an hour later as they came out, "I still have some savings from before we were married, I needn't tell Charles what I paid for it. Let's go have some lunch. The smorgasbord place—I'm mad about their meatballs."

"And that sour-cream dressing with bacon. I've gained three pounds this week already, and I couldn't care less."

"I've gained four. I suppose we'll have to cut down sometime, Laura—the doctor said not over twenty, and we've got four and a half months to go."

"Well, I'm not going to worry about it now," said Laura.

The separate lineups had taken some arranging. Forbes and Katz had gone out to collect their four possibles. Poor ushered Rosalie and Mrs. Keating into the station at four o'clock. They were all interested in the result of this and were all hanging around beside O'Connor and Varallo.

"Now we want you to take your time, Rosalie, and be sure," said Poor. "You understand?"

"Yes, sir. I'll try." Rosalie was subdued, head down beside her mother, who looked anxious.

"This is Lieutenant O'Connor, Rosalie—Detective Varallo. You just take it easy now, there's nothing to be scared of."

"I'm not scared," said Rosalie. She walked ahead of them into the big, bare room on the lower level of the station, where a long platform stretched across one end with the lights ranged on either side and above. A few folding chairs had been set out halfway down. Mrs. Keating and Rosalie sat down, Poor at the girl's other side nodded back at O'Connor. The lights went down.

"Now we just want you to look carefully at all these men, and if you see one you recognize, tell me."

"O.K.," said Rosalie in a small voice.

The first line of men came out on the platform, in the glare of the lights. Chester Kidd was at the far left. They would be off-duty men, jail guards, civilian employees, all picked for general type, size, and age. They were all dressed in casual sports clothes. They stood there, and Rosalie didn't say anything.

"Spot any of them, Rosalie?"

"No, sir."

That line filed off and another came in, with Gregory Silvio in the middle. Rosalie was silent, and just shook her head at Poor. The third line came in, with Samuels at one end, and again she shook her head.

"Take your time, Rosalie. We want you to be sure."

"I am sure."

The fourth line, with Daugherty, stood there, and Rosalie was dumb. To Poor's question she said, "No, sir. It isn't any of those men."

"Are you sure, Rosalie? Absolutely sure?"

"Yes, sir. Really." She raised limpid eyes. "I'd know if I saw him—the right one. None of those men was him."

"All right, Rosalie. Thanks for trying."

In the lobby, Mrs. Keating came up to O'Connor. "You thought it was one of those men, didn't you?"

"All in the day's work," said O'Connor. "We make a lot of false casts."

"Do you think she could be sure? Don't they say there's trauma, or—or just shutting it out of her mind?"

O'Connor gave her his shark's grin. "I don't think the head doctors always know what they're talking about, Mrs. Keating. But I think if she'd seen the right man up there, we'd have got some reaction. And we didn't. Anyway, thanks for coming in."

"And that throws me right back to John's hunch," he added to Varallo when Poor had taken them out. "He's right here, but he isn't in records."

Saturday night, as usual, was busy. Traffic picked up seven drunk drivers between six and midnight. Just after Rhys and Hunter came on, they had a call to a bar out on East Broadway, and found they had a homicide: the bartender was dead. The uniformed men were holding a drunk outside, and various excited patrons told the detectives what had happened. The drunk had tried to pay his check with a hundred-dollar bill, the bartender had objected, and the drunk had pulled a knife. He'd been searched, and the knife was handed over; his name was Carlo Fortelli.

"People," said Rhys. "These temperamental Italians." There would be witnesses coming in to make statements on this, to keep the day watch busy. They took him back and put him in the tank for the night, and started the machinery on the warrant.

An hour later they had a heist at a drugstore. The clerk was a stolid type with sharp eyes, who said he'd know them both again; he gave a good description. Yes, he'd be glad to come down and look at mug shots tomorrow. The heisters had got a good haul in money and drugs.

There was a hit-run out on Glenoaks, with a description of the car but no plate number. After that, nothing showed up for them for a while, and they listened to the Traffic calls until that got boring. Hunter had given up suggesting gin rummy; Rhys wasn't a card player.

At eleven-fifty they had another call; it came through as a rape, and they both went out in a hurry on it. When they got there, at an address on Pioneer, it turned out to be attempted only, but no less interesting for that.

The woman's name was Della Espinoza, and she talked to them excitedly in the living room of this little frame house, cheap furniture and garish curtains but everything neat. She was about thirty, pretty in a heavy way, dark and dramatic. She worked as a waitress at Damon's Steak House downtown.

"So I ask you, how are you going to have it both ways?" she appealed to them. "We got three kids—thank God they're back to sleep now after all the fuss—and they got to be fed, no? My Joe, he's got a good job, he's with this garage, tow service for the auto club, but a couple weeks a month he's on nights—he is now. I don't get home till after eleven. Joe says be careful, and used to be, last year, I'd leave all the yard lights on, not to come home in the dark that late, but who can afford the bill now, I ask you? So I don't turn them on. And tonight this creep was waiting right by the bushes at the back door, he grabs me—"

She was lucky to have got away from him. "But it was a close thing, you bet! He got me by the throat, my God, I'm nearly passed out, he had me on the ground, when I think it's my last breath and I make a big prayer to the Virgin and all of a sudden I remember what she always told me—"

"Er—who?" asked Rhys.

"My mama. Always remember with a man, she says, a knee in the belly or a finger in the eye—and so I bring up my knee good and hard and he lets go just a second, and I kick him and get up and run for the kitchen door, and I think I'll never get the key in but I did, and after I get my breath I call you. Only by then he's gone."

"Well, you were lucky, Mrs. Espinoza. I don't suppose you could describe him?"

"In the dark, fighting for my life? No. But he was a nut. The thing he kept saying, *muy extraño*, you know? While he was wrestling me around. About some girl, some girl named Maggie."

"What? What did he say?"

"It was very funny. He says to me, like this, I didn't hurt Maggie—some name, Watts, Waters—but I'm goin' to hurt you! The only thing he said—in a kind of whisper—"

"Well, I'm damned," said Rhys. " 'I didn't hurt Maggie Walters but I'm going to hurt you.' Like that?"

"That's the name he said, sure, when you said it I remembered. A nut," said Della Espinoza, shrugging.

O'Connor took his blue girl over to Verdugo Park on Sunday morning, where she could get some exercise galloping after a ball without exhausting him as well. There was another man there with a beagle, and a woman with a Peke; they were sitting quietly on benches while the dogs sniffed around. But five minutes after O'Connor arrived things ceased to be quiet, when Maisie got the beagle excited enough to follow her up to the baseball diamond and the Peke followed them and tried to pick a fight with Maisie.

They got the dogs disentangled, and the other dog owners left with indignant remarks, which just showed that big dogs get blamed for everything; it was all the Peke's fault. O'Connor threw the ball until his arm was tired, and sat down to have a cigarette. Maisie galloped all over the baseball diamond at random, and just as he put out the cigarette and reached for the ball again she uttered a scream of joy and flung herself exuberantly on the two Shelties trotting quietly up from the park. They all began to chase each other, and O'Connor turned to face the Shelties' owner apologetically.

"We all told you," said Mary Lou McNally. "Really, Lieutenant—she's wild as a hawk."

"I know," said O'Connor. "I know—but you see, at my job— I just don't have the time."

"Don't make excuses. You can always find time for the things you ought to do," said Mary Lou severely.

"Well, maybe you can." O'Connor felt inferior, which was unusual. He'd first run into Mary Lou, who was twenty, possessed some fantastic I.Q., and was the vice president of the local obedience training club, on that fatal day at the dog show last January when he'd fallen in love with Maisie's mother.

"Two sessions, ten minutes a day, and the regular club meetings Friday nights," said Mary Lou briskly. "In three months you wouldn't know her. You really must."

"Well, I'll think about it," said O'Connor weakly. He had to chase Maisie to get the leash on, and Mary Lou looked disapproving.

When he got home, Katharine said the office had called and he was to call in. O'Connor did.

"So what's new? . . . Jesus H. Christ. You don't say . . . yeah. Yeah, and a couple of things occur to me. I think I'll come in." He went to change from slacks and sweat shirt, and in the garage found Katharine prying open a can. She had her hair tied up and an old smock on. "What are you up to?"

"I'm going to refinish this cradle. It'll look marvelous in antique maple, I told you what a bargain it was."

"Now, Katy—you be careful. I don't think the doctor—"

"I'm fine," said Katharine. "Just fine, darling."

O'Connor and Varallo went to hear Della Espinoza tell it all over again. "Something new," said Varallo. "And interesting. He didn't hurt Maggie. Who ever said he did?"

"And I'll tell you something else that occurs to me, Vic. We said he's cased the women. Just enough to be sure they're alone, or alone sometimes. How the hell has he spotted all these different ones, all over town? Door-to-door salesman he is maybe?"

"Pay your money and take your choice. Unless he's living on welfare, he must have a job—when does he find time? God knows," said Varallo. "But you can think up the time-consuming routine jobs, Charles. Do we go back and ask all the women what door-to-door salesmen they've talked to lately? As if the hospital records weren't enough." Poor and Forbes were back at that.

"Oh hell," said O'Connor. "I guess not. But it makes you wonder."

The drugstore clerk had come in on Sunday morning to look at mug shots, and at eleven o'clock he found one he liked. "That's one of 'em," he said to Katz. "Take my Bible oath on it."

Katz looked at it and said, "That's likely. We're much obliged." The mug shot was of one Stanley Beaver, pedigree back to when he was a J.D., narco, robbery, B. and E., burglary, a lot of counts of narco possession. He was currently on parole from Folsom, and listed at an address in Montrose.

Katz went up there to see if he could find him. It was an old apartment house, like an oven inside—unprecedented for June, the temperature had gone up to a hundred today. The front door of the lower left apartment was open, and after knocking twice Katz pushed it open farther and went in. There was a radio going, loud on rock.

A girl about sixteen was sitting by the window, brushing her long brown hair dreamily. A man who matched the mug shot was stretched out on a filthy day bed, unmoving. Katz went over and shook him. He was dead out: it looked like an O.D.

"Who're you?" asked the girl hazily.

Katz shut off the radio, found a phone and called an ambulance. "What did he take? Is he on pot—speed?"

"Stan? Oh, man, the grass is nothing," she said. "You want some grass? Stan get you some. He fin'lly got hold of some loot last night, get back to the supplier. Got a good fix of H a while ago—"

Too good maybe, thought Katz, waiting for the ambulance. No loss.

On Monday morning, with Poor off, O'Connor was presented with six more names from local hospital records: female babies born in January, February, March, with surnames ending LDMAN. "Goddamn Rex and his infrared snapshots!" he said. They had a parade of witnesses coming in to make statements on that knifing Saturday night.

Varallo was still chasing up old friends of Mrs. Fielding's. "But so far it's damn all, Charles—none of them I've seen had any access to a prescription for Darvon. It's still a little mystery."

"Mystery be damned," said O'Connor crossly, leafing through the reports left on his desk. "Here is one solid fact for you. Burt pinned down the latents you got on that burglary. He was in our records—these stupid goddamned punks—Alfredo Ramirez, pedigree a yard long, still on P.A., an address in Burbank."

"Well, so I'll go see if he's home," said Varallo, and Forbes came in with a yellow Telex sheet.

"How's your blood pressure?" he asked O'Connor. "I kind of hate to give you this. I mean, I wouldn't want you to have a stroke, we're shorthanded as it is."

"So what the hell is it?" O'Connor took it, and a moment later bellowed like a wounded buffalo, on a string of invectives. "Now what the goddamned holy hell is this? Just what—on *Loomis?*"

Varallo reached for the yellow sheet. It was the kickback from the Feds on those dandy prints on the glass bookend. The Feds had identified them. They belonged to Elizabeth Ann Harris, twenty-four six years ago, Caucasian, five-five, a hundred and twenty, blond and blue, no marks or scars. The pedigree was a fairly long one, going back to a juvenile record: narco possession, soliciting, con (badger game), all in and around Chicago. She'd served petty sentences, thirty days, sixty days, and had last been heard of when she got off probation in Joliet, Illinois five and a half years ago.

"On Loomis?" roared O'Connor. "That—that—"

"Stuffed shirt," said Varallo. "*Non dubiti*, Charles. She was soliciting door to door and Loomis lectured her about her morals and she biffed him one. But what the hell indeed? This is wild all right."

# EIGHT

"Wild?" said O'Connor. "Wild? It's lunatic!" He looked at the Telex as if it were a rattlesnake. "I don't believe it! Harris—a goddamned tart from Chicago!"

"Fairly offbeat," said Varallo, "but human, Charles—human. Because you know what it says." Rereading the salient features of Elizabeth Ann, he started to laugh.

"I know what I said at the time," said Forbes. "Anybody can change his pattern. And this Loomis was just too good to be true. Little Goody Two-Shoes. So now we find out he was human, like Vic says. He picked this girl up somewhere—or vice versa—and took her home. Had a fight with her—or vice versa."

"Joliet!" said O'Connor.

"People move around. We can't even guess where he met her. I don't suppose Loomis would have dropped into a bar, and we don't have many bars here where the owners welcome the B-girls. But you know the type this Harris must be. They take jobs on and off when the pickings are slim—could be she's a waitress somewhere he went, even a market checker. Anyway, somehow they got together."

"Loomis," said O'Connor, and suddenly began to laugh. "Oh, my God, I see it, and I tell you, boys, it restores my faith in the essential silliness of human nature. That ultra-respectable moral man—the feet of clay like anybody else. But of all the damned outlandish things—"

"If we can ever drop on her, we may hear a blow-by-blow account," said Varallo amusedly, "but we can speculate some. Say on that Friday or Saturday night he decided to go out to dinner, somewhere besides a health-food counter, and she picked

him up—there or somewhere else. Came home with him, and can
we guess—the bed was all neatly made up—got into an argument
about the price? Could be Harris has a little temper, and got
mad when he tried to beat her down."

O'Connor burst out laughing again. "Well, however you read
it, it's the goddamndest thing! It's got to be something like that,
whatever happened, however it did happen—and the family'll
never believe it, you know. With this Harris' prints on that
thing—my God, talk about an offbeat one! And not one damn
lead where to look—he could have been anywhere, picked her up
at a disco in Hollywood or—or a five and dime."

"Human nature, you can say," said Forbes. "Everything we
turned up on him, I don't think he'd ever talked to anybody
even had a moving-violation ticket, much less a pedigree."

"But the pedigree could be useful," Varallo pointed out. "Evidently Harris has stayed out of trouble for a while, but that
kind don't change. All the Feds tell us is that she's on record—
Illinois will have more, mug shots and chapter and verse. Could
be she followed a man out here, even has relatives. Let's ask—
that may give us a handle."

"She could even be operating a grade above what she was,
as a call girl," suggested Forbes. "Why'd you think of an argument about money?"

"Because of the double lock," said Varallo, grinning. "We can
deduce that she has a temper. Loomis' billfold was there, with
money in it—how much, Charles?"

"Little over fifty bucks. I see what you mean," and O'Connor
was laughing again.

"And the spring lock in the knob was turned. Whatever set
off Harris' temper, she hit him with the bookend—not meaning
to kill him, probably—and ran out, before she thought to lift
any cash or other loot. The door slammed and she couldn't get
back in. Not only after any loot, but to wipe off her prints, if
she remembered that at all."

"And this is the funniest damned thing we've run across this
year," said O'Connor. "But we'd better have a try at finding her,

if anybody can give us a lead. My God—Loomis and a third-rate twist like that—we'll see if Joliet can tell us anything." He was still laughing as he started down to Communications.

It was about the last answer they had expected on Loomis, but at least it was an answer. And one like Harris could be anywhere; a look at the details of her record might give them an idea where to look.

But as Varallo started over to Burbank to see if he could pick up the burglar, he was still grinning; in a way, as Charles said, it was refreshing to know that there was nothing new about human nature.

At the address they had for Alfredo Ramirez, he raised a fat girl in her teens who told him that Papa wasn't home. She didn't know when he would be home.

Considering his record, the family was probably familiar with the smell of cop. It wasn't worth staking out. Varallo came back to base and sent a query to D.M.V. in Sacramento about any car registered to that address. D.M.V. replied within the hour: Ramirez had no driver's license, no car, but there was a Pontiac registered to Mrs. Consuelo Ramirez of the same address, plate number appended. Varallo put out an A.P.B. on the car and Ramirez.

As a matter of routine Katz checked the hospital to find out if Stan Beaver had died. He hadn't; eventually he'd be transferred to jail. The girl could be questioned. Katz didn't know whether she might end up sharing the robbery charge, but she had to be talked to; he went and collected her and brought her back for questioning. She was sullen and scared and talked reluctantly.

"I don't know where he got the bread. Maybe somebody owed him. What the hell business is it of cops? Or if he wants to take a fix?" She parted with her name grudgingly, Jimmie Lou Grubbs. It wasn't anybody's business where she was from, or whether she had any family; she could take care of herself.

She couldn't be over sixteen. Katz felt tired, thinking of what was ahead of her.

He'd applied for a search warrant yesterday, and it came through about noon. He and Forbes went up to that Montrose apartment and looked around. Neither of them was much interested in the dopies: it was just a job. Forbes was still tickled about the Loomis thing, and they speculated on what might have happened there.

"I could quote the wisdom of Solomon," said Katz. *"The thing which hath been, it is that which shall be."*

They found a plastic bag with some high-grade marijuana in its bottom, and a couple of ounces of much-cut H, some miscellaneous pills. There were a few clothes in the one closet, and they went through pockets automatically. In the torn lining of a ragged sports jacket Katz found a single scrap of paper with a barely legible scrawl on it: *Roddy No-1-6424.* "Well, I do wonder," said Katz. "She did say, he'd just got back to the supplier. It's an L.A. prefix, we'll see if the boys downtown recognize this one." When they'd turned in the evidence at the station, he called the Narco Bureau at LAPD and passed on the gist of the scrawl to a Captain Goldfarb.

"Say anything? It sure as hell does," said Goldfarb. "Roddy Esteban—pedigree with us way back. We'd wondered if he was dealing again, he's just off P.A. We'll have a look, thanks for the tip."

"Well, if he is, he had at least one client in Glendale and probably more," said Katz. "If you come up with any names belonging over here, we'd like to know."

"Sure thing."

Katz was still sitting there talking about Loomis with Forbes when a Telex came in from Sacramento. O'Connor had asked D.M.V. about any car registered to the Harris woman. There wasn't any.

Nothing came in from Joliet at all. Wayne and Varallo were out looking in hospital records in the Burbank hospitals.

At four o'clock Goldfarb called back. "We just missed Roddy —he saw us coming and went out the back. Not that it's any loss, he left all his stuff behind him. He was dealing again all right—quite a lot of stuff."

"And he'll be back in business tomorrow," said Katz. "Why do we bother?"

"I sometimes wonder. Anyway, among the stuff he left was a notebook—we deduce, a list of clients. No names, just phone numbers. About two dozen prefixes belonging to your territory. You want those, I suppose."

"To check out and go see if they're holding. It's one of the things we're paid for."

"Well, I'll send a Xerox copy over. No hurry?"

"No hurry in the world," said Katz. "Thanks very much." As he put the phone down he felt his nose. The bandage had come off yesterday, and it felt all right: still a little tender.

On Tuesday morning Varallo went out with the few names they'd got from the Burbank hospital records—clearing up as they went. He could foresee how this one was going to end: this was a forlorn piece of routine that would use up a lot of time and get them nowhere in the end. They would, in time, get through all the birth records in the county, if O'Connor decided to go on with it, and it would give them damn all on the identity of those kids. But while they were working it, it had to be checked as they went.

Nothing had come in from Joliet yet.

Most of the new addresses were in Burbank. He saw a Mrs. Oldman and her baby at a very new, expensive house up in the hills, and a Mrs. Wildman and her baby in a cramped apartment out by Lockheed. He saw a Mrs. Coldman and her baby in one side of a duplex on Alameda, and a Mrs. Poldman and her baby in a tiny rented house behind a larger house on Cordova Street. The heat wave, mercifully, was subsiding; it was only in the low nineties today.

It was getting on for noon when he found the address listed for Mrs. William Waldman, female baby born March 31 at St. Joseph's. It was an old, narrow street of old single houses, a sleazy, down-at-heel block in an old section of town, Blakely Court. Few of the yards were kept up; most of the houses needed painting.

There was parking only on one side; he spotted the address, walked across the street, and shoved the doorbell. There were no curtains at the windows; the place looked empty. He tried the house on the left, where there was a semblance of green lawn, and a young woman with her hair in fat curlers answered the door and told him they didn't know any of the neighbors, they'd just moved in. He tried the house on the right.

It was a cracker-box stucco place, scabrous tan, and the woman who answered the door was mountainously fat, with platinum blond hair and a grotesque mask of make-up, twin spots of rouge and a blob of carmine mouth. She had on a pink cotton dress and not much else, he thought, and her incongruously tiny bare feet had the toenails painted to match her lipstick.

"The Waldmans? What about 'em?" she asked.

"Have they moved? Do you know where they went?"

"How would I know? I'm not their keepers. You from Mr. Griswold?"

"No," said Varallo. "Who's that?"

She relaxed. "Landlord. That man can find more to complain about—and money-hungry, he's the world's worst. What you want with the Waldmans?"

"It's just a matter of checking hospital records," said Varallo vaguely. "It seems there might be a discrepancy and Mrs. Waldman may have some money coming back."

"Well, just fancy that. It'd be that fifty bucks Bill had to pay to get her in—he was mad about that, they thought the welfare'd pay it all."

"Do you know where they moved, Mrs.—"

"Geyer. Mrs. Elmira Geyer, that's me. Well, I don't know for sure—they wouldn't 've gone anywhere, but that fella from Mr. Griswold was so nasty, making a fuss about the rent, so they took off. Alice, she said something to me, couple of days before, about them maybe goin' up to stay with Bill's brother up in a place called Grover City."

"I see. Were there any other children besides the baby?"

"Oh, they got two boys too. Little kids."

And that was just enough of a lead to follow up. Varallo stopped for lunch, went back to the station and found O'Connor poring over a couple of Telex sheets. "Don't tell me that's something from Joliet on Harris? Finally?"

"And it doesn't give us one damn thing," said O'Connor. "The ones like Harris—my God, Vic. A dime a dozen in any city in the country. How many of 'em in any city in the country? Take a look!" He flung the sheets over.

The pedigree didn't say much, certainly. The petty record behind her when she was picked up there the last time, on a prostitution charge. She'd run with a lot of men, but no one permanently; she had casual acquaintances among the ones like herself. There wasn't any indication of why she might have headed for California, if there had been any reason—or if she hadn't just landed here the week before she met Loomis. Somehow. "Was there a mug shot with this?"

O'Connor grunted at it, shoved it over with one finger. "What could it say either?"

"*E vero*," said Varallo sadly. It hadn't been taken to flatter the subject, and it didn't. The wire transmission hadn't improved its quality. It showed a square-faced young woman with dirty blond hair drawn over her ears, scanty eyebrows and a thin, sullen mouth; her skin looked blotched in the glare of the lights police photographers used. But superimpose on it in imagination the make-up, the curled and dressed hair, the inviting smile, it only said that this was a candid photograph. It told nothing of the woman at all; not, probably, that there was much interesting to know. Varallo put it down. "Where is Grover City, Charles?"

"How should I know? Why?"

"One of our possible surnames may have gone there. Escaping the landlord." Varallo looked in the atlas and found it, a dot on the map two hundred miles up the coast in San Luis Obispo County. "I don't suppose there's a police force. Probably in the sheriff's jurisdiction." He went down to Communications and sent a Telex up there to the sheriff: Were the William Waldmans there, said to be staying with his relatives in Grover City, surname probably the same. If so, were any children with them?

"I think Richard Loomis is going to sue us," said O'Connor when he came back. "He called just now and I told him what we'd come up with. He nearly frothed at the mouth. We're a bunch of nitwits to think that Barney would ever have had anything to do with such a woman. My God, Vic, could there have been some goddamn silly mistake about those prints, the Feds getting them mixed up with somebody else's?"

"Just because it's offbeat, don't look for excuses, Charles." The phone light flashed, and he picked up the phone. "Varallo."

"That A.P.B. on your burglar," said Duff. "Traffic just picked him up."

"Well, a step further on."

"It was just by accident. Kogan got called to a family dispute and spotted the car outside."

"More luck than good management."

"He's bringing him in now."

Varallo went down to meet Kogan in the black-and-white, to collect Alfredo Ramirez and book him in at the jail. "I called up a tow car," said Kogan. "The Pontiac had a lot of stuff in the back, fur coat, tape recorder, portable radio—could be part of the loot."

"What about it, Ramirez?" asked Varallo.

Ramirez just looked unhappy and didn't say. "I shoulda had more sense then to come back to Glendale, but I wanted to see my kid. My Stefano. It's his name day and I hadda present for him."

It could be deduced, the loot still on him, Ramirez's tame fence had got dropped on or gone out of business otherwise. But Varallo suddenly remembered something else, and as he shepherded Ramirez over to the jail, he asked, "That place you knocked over last Saturday night—didn't you notice the signs on the doors?"

"What signs? Oh, sure, I seen them little stickers sort of things. Why, what were they?" Like any professional, Ramirez was taking his capture fairly philosophically: all in the day's work.

"Didn't you read them?"

Ramirez looked apologetic. "Well, I tell you how it is," he said. "I don't read the English, mister. Not nohow."

It was so simple when you knew, thought Varallo.

Just before the end of shift he had a long-distance call from a Steve Babcock, who introduced himself as the Chief of Police of a place called Arroyo Grande. "We got your Telex about these Waldmans. Grover City's in our territory. Would the relatives be James and Norman Waldman?"

"I've got no idea," said Varallo. "Could be."

"We've got a record on James, a 502. You just want to know if these people are here, that's all? With their kids?"

"That's all. Two little boys and a baby."

"O.K. We'll have a look." The chief didn't ask why they wanted to know, politely staying out of what wasn't his business, but he sounded a little curious.

On Wednesday, with the temperature down to a reasonable eighty-four, Varallo finished spraying and feeding the rest of his roses, and discovered with some excitement that there was a first tiny bud on Pedrálbes. Mr. Anderson was out in his yard next door, and Varallo called him over to see it; Mr. Anderson was something of a rose man too.

"Should be really something to see, a chartreuse one."

They were still looking at it when Laura came out, looking cool and charming in a blue halter sundress, and asked if she could take the Gremlin. "Where are you off to? Seems to me you're gadding around too much. Well, if you'll remember to pick up some cigarettes for me, sure."

"Just to lunch with Katharine," said Laura. "She's discovered a wonderful new French place in La Cañada. Thanks, darling, I'll be home about three."

"—And another heist by these damned females," Katz was saying as Varallo came in on Thursday morning. "Though that's the least of it, nothing to do on it. You missed a dull day, Vic, but the night watch made up for it. We've got a new A.P.B. on a hit-run and another derelict D.O.A. picked up on the steps at the public library, and two heists at opposite ends of town."

"In the middle of the week?" said Varallo, yawning.

"What's the day to the punks any more? John and Fred are out on the heists. No kind of description, one was a citizen in a parking lot and the other a bar, so damned dark you couldn't recognize your own mother," said O'Connor. "I swear to God, Vic, when I think what a quiet little place this used to be—"

"And just look at what LAPD's sent me," said Katz. He handed Varallo a Xeroxed sheet: a list of phone numbers, all with local prefixes. "That supplier had built up quite a little clientele here, it seems, and now we'll have to check all these out, damn it. Waste time on the holding charges, any we find, and all the paperwork on it—God." He snorted.

"Nobody twisted your arm to carry the badge, Joe." The phone light went on. "Yes, Al?"

"I've got a call for you from a Mrs. Corbett at a convalescent home."

"Oh? All right, put her on . . ." That thing still intrigued him: maybe a little thing, but a real mystery. He wondered if Mrs. Corbett had discovered a clue. But all she said was, "I've got all the records for you, Mr. Varallo, the exact amounts of all the Darvon in our stock for the week before and after Mrs. Fielding died. Dr. Norenberg asked us to make a separate copy for you."

"Well, if he's seen it and is satisfied—"

"No, Mr. Varallo, he was most insistent that the police have a copy. I've got it all ready for you, if you'll just ask at the office Miss Dassett has it."

"O.K., thanks," said Varallo. "Which heist do I get, Charles?"

"John's at the hospital with the one got knifed—oh, didn't you hear that? The one in the parking lot—but Fred'll likely need some help sorting out the witnesses from the bar."

"Has that chief of police called back from Arroyo Grande?"

"Where the hell is that?" asked Katz.

"I haven't heard." O'Connor sounded surly; but Varallo had seen the story in the *News-Press* last night, the predictably cute human-interest story about the female Robin Hoods, and he was aware that O'Connor was merely annoyed at whatever reporter had belatedly put it in print.

He went down to the Broad Heights Convalescent Home; easier to pick up that report and file it away than argue either with Mrs. Corbett or Norenberg. But there wouldn't be anything in it suggestive of where or how Bertha Fielding had come by the enormous overdose. If there had been any discrepancy in the convalescent home's supply, it would have come to light before this.

He was abstractly glad he didn't have to go down those corridors, or face Miss Dorothy Dilbeck again. He wondered how the new roommate liked her. He went into the receptionist's office, the door open today, and said, "My name's Varallo—Mrs. Corbett left a report for me."

"Oh yes, sir, she said a police officer would be in." She was a toothy girl with glasses; she looked at him with frank curiosity and admiration. "I'll get it for you, sir."

She had been typing, the desk pulled out at right angles to the main desk, and as he waited there he glanced idly at the long account form in the machine. It was headed MONTHLY STATE-MENT, and below that MR. EDWARD RANSOME, 5/30–6/31. Ransome was right, thought Varallo, looking at the figures below. When she came back he said, "Excuse me, I just noticed—would this be the average monthly charge here?"

She was pleased to answer any questions. "Yes, sir, it's a standard charge—thirty-eight dollars a day for a two-bed room, thirty-four for four-bed. Well, no, sir, that doesn't cover everything, of course—the doctor is paid separately, and there's the bill for any medication. That comes direct from the pharmacy to whoever's paying the bill, you see."

Not a racket, maybe: they'd have to pay all these nurses and aides a pretty good salary, of course, there'd be the cooks and janitors, the laundry. "What would the medication run to?"

"Well, it depends what the patient's getting, but of course a lot of them are on prescriptive medication that runs as high as seventy, eighty a month. Why, no, sir, there's not much difference in prices, most convalescent homes charge about the same. Would you like to see Mrs. Corbett, sir?"

"No, no, that's all right, thanks." Varallo took the manila envelope she handed him. *Dio*, he thought, that was a piece of money; but probably he and all the other taxpayers were paying it, via Medicare and the state programs.

He didn't look at the report. When he got back to the station, Wayne had brought in four witnesses to the heist at the bar, and he took statements from two of them.

He had just got the second citizen's signature on that and noticed that it was a quarter to twelve when Duff buzzed him. "It's long distance for you, from Arroyo Grande."

"Yes. Babcock? Varallo. What have you got?"

"Just what's your interest in these Waldmans, anyway? I only ask out of curiosity."

Arroyo Grande was paying for the call; Varallo told him. "It's the hell of a long way round, you can see, and ten to one it'll give us nothing at all. But it's the only smell of a lead we've got on identifying those bodies." He was rather surprised at getting no comment on the enormity of those bodies, the kids, the baby. Maybe rural cops saw as much of the blood, the mess, the dirt as city cops, come to think. "This is just a first cast, covering local hospitals. Did you find the Waldmans?"

"Oh, we found 'em," said Babcock. "Mr. and Mrs. William, in a trailer park down by the beach, with his brother Jim. The 502. Of course I didn't know the background on this. That is a thing, Varallo. Quite a thing. But you asked about the kids. No kids visible, so I asked. They're said to be with Mrs. Waldman's sister down your way. A Mrs. Celia Spears, I got the address for you—Coronado Street, L.A."

"Thanks very much, we'll check that."

"Welcome," said Babcock. "It isn't often we can help out the big city."

Some time today, he'd follow that up. But they were a little busy until the middle of the afternoon. Katz, swearing at the necessity, had been onto the phone company, and they'd come up with a partial list of names to match those phone numbers, were working on the rest. He and Wayne had gone out and fetched in three of Esteban's clients, all picked up with the grass, speed, one with a little supply of H, and were busy at all the paperwork on that.

It wasn't until four o'clock that Varallo said, "Damnation, these Waldmans—I'd better check it out just to be thorough. That's about the last of the local hospital records, Charles, unless you want to tackle every single hospital in L. A. County."

"Is it worth it?—damn it, Vic, I think so. Probabilities—damn it, I'd like to get somebody for that, and unless we can find out who the kids were— Look, we've got LAPD right next door and they're always co-operative, we can ask to borrow a computer and program it to pick out the right records." O'Connor sat back from the typewriter, scowling; there was ink all over his fingers where he'd been struggling with the ribbon, and his jowl was blue with beard. "I'll get onto Captain Grayson, I know him, and see if we can set it up."

At least the heat wave was gone. Varallo looked at the county guide—Coronado Street was down in the middle of L.A., near the Civic Center—and got the Gremlin's tank filled before he got on the freeway.

"Alice's kids?" said Celia Spears blankly. She was an emaciated young woman in jeans and a halter top; Varallo had interrupted her as she watched TV over a can of beer and pretzels. The place was a run-down duplex on a side street. "What in hell would Alice's kids be doing here? I've got three too many of my own to look after, mister. Who told you Alice's kids were here?"

"She did."

"Well, she's nuts. I always said so. Catch me stay married to a drunk like that. No, I haven't seen her lately—my car's been on the fritz, and we're not too buddy-buddy anyways. What's this all about?"

"When did you see your sister's children last?" asked Varallo.

"Oh, who remembers? I don't know—couple of months ago, maybe."

"Maybe your husband would remember more—"

She looked at him incredulously. "Husband? Who's got a husband, for God's sake? I got a husband, I don't get the welfare for the kids!"

Varallo called Chief Babcock back at five-thirty but he'd already left the office, said a deputy. "This is Varallo down in Glendale. He knows all about it—would you just ask him to do some more checking. The Waldmans look possible, and we'd be obliged if he'd talk to them again. I'll call him in the morning."

On Thursday night, in contrast to Wednesday, Rhys and Hunter didn't have any calls until nine o'clock. Then they had a call from Traffic, a homicide, and both went out on it. It was an address on Highland.

Stoner had been on it first, and he was an experienced man but he was looking sick and shaken. "It's—I never saw anything like this," he said. "I think she's got to be nuts."

It was a nice house. There was a corpse in the living room, a middle-aged woman with a butcher knife in her chest, staring mutely at the ceiling. There was a queer-looking teen-age girl sitting on the couch, and Stoner had put the cuffs on her. Rhys was shocked.

"My God, you shouldn't have done that—a juvenile, and just what the hell happened here?"

"I had to, she was over there at the neighbors' with another knife, after the kids," said Stoner. "I don't know what the hell, except that she's nuts. I gather that's her mother."

Feeling a little shaken too, Rhys and Hunter went over to the neighbors'. The neighbor told them that the two children had run over screaming, and she'd locked the door. "I knew it would come to something like this—I knew it! That girl! Trying to poison Sammy—"

The little girl was too young to talk to, but the boy was ten, a smart boy. Still scared, but speaking up. "When she did that to Mama, I just grabbed up Carla and ran—over here, I told Mrs. Nichols to call you—if Dad had been home he'd have stopped her, but he hadda go to 'Frisco on that lawsuit—you gotta call him, please—"

They made one attempt to question the girl, the queer-looking girl, brown hair in a veil over her eyes. She didn't even raise her head, just sat there, not struggling against the cuffs, and she said, "She told me to go to bed. I didn't want to go to bed. She won't try to boss me again."

"My God," said Rhys. "My God." The neighbors told them the name was Finch, and there'd been some trouble with the law already.

At eleven-fifty Sergeant Harrison answered a call. "Is Mr. Poor there?" asked an agitated female voice.

"No, ma'am, Detective Poor's on day watch. Can I help you?"

"I—this is Mrs. Keating. I have to report—my daughter's missing. Rosalie Keating. She—I thought she might be with a friend, but—"

"How old is she, Mrs. Keating?"

"Fifteen. She—I really would like to talk to Mr. Poor, he knows all about it—or Lieutenant O'Connor. Please, if you could—because it must be something to do with that—"

Harrison's mind suddenly made connections. He knew about that rapist, of course, and the lineups. He said, "Now take it easy, Mrs. Keating. I'll call the lieutenant and tell him. Meanwhile, you tell me her description and what she had on, and we'll get it on the air."

Gideon Algernon Cadwallader pounced at Varallo's glass, and having finished the brandy-and-soda Varallo tipped an ice cube out for him. "Those Waldmans," he said thoughtfully.

"It's just too much, about those children," said Laura. Her bright brown head was bent over a piece of embroidery. "You can't imagine a thing like that—how or why. In a civilized world."

"But it's not, very," said Varallo ruefully. "As any cop knows, *cara*." He looked at her, thinking about the new baby (maybe idiots to do it, in this uncivilized twentieth-century world) and about his darling Ginevra, and he thought suddenly of Rupert Fielding saying, *Fifty-five years*. He wondered how he and Laura would be after that many years, and—thinking about that place— it was a nightmarish thought, because he'd be eighty-eight and Laura eighty-five, and it was such a ridiculous idea that they could ever be that old, he suddenly laughed.

"I meant to tell you," said Laura, holding her needle to the light and squinting at it, "I priced that carpet for the nursery. We can't afford it, Vic. It's fifteen dollars a yard, and the cheaper ones aren't worth buying, they wouldn't wear a year. I'd rather make do with an area rug. Of course everything is expensive now, but I thought—"

"*Diavolo!*" said Varallo suddenly. "*Capperì!*"

"What?" said Laura.

Varallo got up. He said slowly, "I wonder. *Facciamo la spese secondo l'entrata.* Cut the coat according to the cloth. And isn't that the truth."

"What's hit you?" asked Laura.

"Something . . . I think I'll just go and ask," said Varallo gently.

# NINE

The house was all dark. Varallo pushed the bell three, four, five times, and waited nearly ten minutes before the inner bolt was drawn slowly back. The door opened halfway. "Mr. Fielding. Varallo, headquarters. I'd like to talk to you again."

"Oh—yes," said Fielding. "All right. Come in. Just a moment." He fumbled at a switch, and a low-wattage bulb went on in the entry hall. His tall, stooping figure turned in the shadows, led Varallo down the step into the bare living room; he switched on another lamp, scarcely brighter than the first. "Sit down. What did you want to ask?"

"We hadn't asked," said Varallo, "because it didn't look relevant, Mr. Fielding. I just thought about it a while ago—about the money. It occurred to me to wonder whether Medicare or one of the state programs was paying—but when you have an independent income, as Dr. Norenberg told us, I suppose they weren't?"

Fielding sat down heavily in a big armchair across the room. "Oh no," he said. "No. I should have realized it wouldn't be put down to some convenient blunder—that's such an efficient place, isn't it? I'm only sorry—about Louise. For Louise."

"Mr. Fielding?"

"You don't," said Fielding, "want a lecture on the fallacies of socialism. You guessed about it—you know, don't you, once you thought about the money."

"You could put it that way. You had money, so no agency was picking up the tab."

"Oh, dear me, no, it's nothing as logical as that," said Fielding with a rather ghastly smile. "I always made good money, and

I invested it. I got out of real estate, because I'd got burned in that during the war, with rents frozen and taxes up, and I could see another round of that eventually. Almost anything's a gamble now, but the stock market had been fairly steady—I thought it was safer then—it's all in mutual funds. A good retirement income, on almost a hundred and fifty thousand—fifteen hundred a month I'd arranged for in the regular withdrawal plan."

"And then your wife had to go into the convalescent home."

"That's right. We'd been paying into Medicare for years, and the state program too—you never find out about these things until something happens, do you? They didn't pay anything at all, not even part of it," said Fielding, "because she didn't need skilled nursing. Only waiting on round the clock, but not *skilled* nursing—that's the way the rules read. It paid the first week in the home, and then nothing."

"And the money's been draining away month by month," said Varallo softly.

"Oh, something more—more fundamental than that. There was a backlog of savings—at first—but the doctor wanted X rays, a whole series of tests—and prices began going up so fast. The monthly bills—they were seldom under thirteen hundred, what with the medication, the doctor. And the market—you know what's been happening. It was"— Fielding was shaking his head slowly from side to side—"like being caught in a trap— nothing I could do. Nothing. The mutual funds—they'd been having to sell capital stock to meet the monthly withdrawals, and I couldn't tell the broker to cut that down, I had to have it to pay the bills. I never told Louise, to worry her. She knew the bill at the nursing home was taking most of my income, but not about—the other. She earns just about enough for herself at her job. And we had to live—here. Food to buy, the taxes, the utilities are all so high now—she's a good girl, and she's helped with that. We sold some of the antiques—that carried us through several months, and the oriental rugs—I never told Bertha that, it would have grieved her. I never told her how it was about the capital."

"What happened two weeks ago, Mr. Fielding?"

"It worried me dreadfully, that there'd be nothing to leave Louise—that it would all be gone in a little while. After all I'd saved, all I'd planned. Just draining away—the capital getting sold off—and nothing I could do. Nothing else I could buy into that would pay that income—and if I sold what was left, it would be at a seventy-five per cent loss, what I'd paid. The broker said—but there was nothing I could do. Take the cash for the remaining stock, it would have paid the bills for six months—and after that, nothing. Bertha couldn't have stayed there—she'd have been on the welfare rolls, some state place —or if we'd brought her home, Louise would have had to quit her job, and she couldn't take care of her twenty-four hours a day, and a nurse—if we could get one—about the cheapest, four, five, six dollars an hour. It was—a trap," said Fielding. "A trap."

"So what did you do?" asked Varallo.

"She wanted to go, but she'd never have done it herself—she was a religious woman. I decided," said Fielding painfully, "that if there was any sin involved, I would take it on myself. It was the last kindness I could do for her, to see she went— easy and quiet—while she was still in that nice place, looked after so well. To see her out of her pain. She'd have hated— being a public charge. I'd have hated it for her." He looked up slowly. "Dr. Norenberg—everybody—making such a mystery, how it happened. When it was so simple. When Bertha went into the convalescent home two years ago, the doctor had just given her that prescription for Darvon. I hadn't got it filled yet, and he didn't ask for it—we both forgot it. After that, all the prescriptions went through the nursing home. But I found it— just that week—and it came to me, it was the only thing to do, you see. The last thing I could do. I got it filled, and I emptied all the capsules into a little water in the medicine bottle. And that last afternoon—"

"Yes, you always stayed and helped her with her dinner, you said."

"Yes. And before Louise got there, that day, I just put it in Bertha's tea," said Fielding simply. "She always finished the whole pot, and she liked it very sweet, so if there was any taste —but she didn't say anything. It was the last of her special Lapsang Souchong. She didn't know anything about it, and you don't want to think Louise knew anything. I was surprised I didn't—even feel anything special, anything wrong or even very sad. We said good night, and I kissed her, and she said—she said everybody was too good to a useless old woman—and Louise and I came home. I knew the doctor would call in the morning." He was silent, and then he said, "It was queer—I didn't feel anything at all until after the funeral. Then—it seemed so strange, as if everything had come to an end. No routine to the day— nowhere to go."

"Mr. Fielding, you know you'll have to come with me, now you've told me all this."

"I know," said Fielding submissively. "I know. It'll be a terrible shock to Louise. I'll have to tell her—before we leave. I wonder if you'd just call her down." He gave Varallo the travesty of a smile. "Oh, you needn't be afraid to leave me. I haven't anything to take—to commit suicide. I rather wish I had, it'd be the easiest way."

As Varallo hesitated there, before deciding to call up a squad car just to be on the safe side, it all passed through his mind, the anticlimaxes to this little drama. He'd be charged with voluntary manslaughter, and the newspapers would have headlines about mercy killings; the odds were against his living out any sentence, and the daughter would be tagged from now on as part of a sensational case.

If Loomis had illustrated that human nature remained constant for lust and greed, Fielding might illustrate it as constant for love and kindness: or was it, thought Varallo sadly, just that he'd been ashamed to lose all the money, unable to take care of his own?

Either way, it was a little mess.

With talking to the daughter at the station, and booking Fielding into jail, he was there past eleven o'clock. Tomorrow start the paperwork on it, apply for the warrant.

The night watch was out on a new homicide. That was all they needed.

When he got home, Laura was in bed; she stirred and sat up and switched on the light. "Now, may I hear where you went dashing off to, on what?"

"A brainstorm I wish I hadn't had," said Varallo, taking off his jacket. "Why the hell did Norenberg have to be so fussy about cause of death? If he'd just let it lay, a lot of unhappiness avoided. *Gli pazzli crescono senza in affiarli.*"

"What are you talking about?"

"Human nature," said Varallo.

When he got in on Friday morning, a general air of hectic busyness was in the air. O'Connor and Poor were at the coffee machine in the hall, both unshaven and disheveled, and told him about Rosalie. They'd been up half the night, said O'Connor, out hunting the damned girl, and why the hell she should run off like that—

"I can't help feeling it's my fault, damn it," said Poor. "That lineup must have been an ordeal for a kid like that. After what she'd been through—"

"But why the hell should she run away?" O'Connor drank black coffee thirstily. "And where could she go? The mother thought, that girl friend, but that was N.G. The other closest friend she had moved away last year—" They had canvassed everybody Rosalie knew at school, all her teachers: every squad car in town had been on the lookout.

"Oh, Mr. Poor—" They all looked around. It was Virginia Waters, trim in her blue blouse and skirt, looking troubled. "I just came on and heard about Rosalie. You haven't found her yet? Why did she run away—she did, didn't she?"

"We don't know. Her mother was out last night, says Rosalie

was just as usual when she left, and gone when she came home. It doesn't look as if she'd made any plans, she didn't take any clothes, and her mother says she couldn't have had over five dollars. It's just senseless," said Poor worriedly. "Would you have any ideas?—you talked to her."

Virginia shook her head. "That poor kid! I wonder what's behind it."

"She's bound to turn up," said Varallo. "She can't have got far on five bucks, and with her description out—I heard we've got a new homicide."

"Oh, my God," said O'Connor, "and is Joe going to be interested in that." This was Katz's day off. "He said we'd hear more about that psycho girl—the one that tried to poison the dog. She stabbed her mother to death last night. We haven't contacted the father yet, he's in 'Frisco. Bob was nervous about stashing her in our jail, and sent her over to the guarded wing at Emergency, for which I don't blame him. And we've got these Nichols coming in to make statements on that—the neighbors —and until we can locate the father, who's going to take care of the other kids God knows."

"And you haven't heard about Fielding." Varallo poured himself a cup of coffee and followed them back to the office to tell them about that. Wayne was on the phone, Forbes swearing at his typewriter. "The little mystery solved—so simple when you know, and I'm sorry for that poor devil."

"God," said O'Connor in comment. "If Norenberg hadn't got all fussed about it—and what the hell did it matter, anyway? Not as if the old man was going to do it again to somebody else. As it is, he'll have to be charged and tried, it'll make headlines— and hell for the daughter—and what's the odds in the end? He'll use what money he's got left paying a lawyer."

"And I wonder," said Poor morosely, "how many poor devils are in exactly the same bind, Mama or Papa or Grandpa eating up the cash in those homes. I never have understood that prayer against sudden death. I'd rather have it that way any time—it's cleaner."

"And cheaper," said O'Connor cynically. He switched on the radio on his desk to the Traffic calls. "Goddamn that girl, where's she got to?"

Wayne put down the phone. "I just got hold of Robert Finch in 'Frisco. He's taking the first plane down. And wasn't Joe right, saying that that head doctor was a fool—if they'd had that girl locked up, this could never have happened. The hell of it is, you can't say they weren't warned, the trouble they'd already had with her. What Bob got from the neighbors last night—"

The phone light flashed on Varallo's desk and he reached for the phone. "Varallo."

"This is Babcock. I thought you'd like to know you can quit all the legwork on your bodies. Even before you called back last night, I was feeling interested enough, what you'd told me, to chase up Waldman again. We picked him up on a drunk charge about midnight, and I asked him a few questions. We sometimes take a few shortcuts where it's indicated," and Babcock's voice was bland. "Oh, I told him all about his rights, but I don't know if he took it in."

"You don't mean—"

"Oh, he knew what he was saying—just, if he'd been strictly sober, he might not have said it to me." Babcock chuckled without humor. "I asked him where the kids were, and he said they were a goddamned nuisance and he'd got rid of them for good."

"*Diavolo!*" said Varallo. "He admitted—"

"As good as. There may be a few loose ends but you can tie them up. I take it you'll want him—and the wife. I wonder if she knew about it," said Babcock. "I haven't talked to her. You'll be getting a warrant."

"My good God in heaven," said Varallo. "I know we see the dirt at the bottom, but—"

"Sometimes it's a little muckier than usual," said Babcock dryly. "It'll make an excuse for a ride down to the city. If you'll have a warrant to show me, say by the middle of the afternoon, I'll be there to hand 'em over."

"Do I say thanks? We'd be obliged—we are obliged. But—

well, I said it's not all that civilized a world. My God. We'll expect you . . . Charles, we just hit a jackpot. And you can thank
Burt for the painstaking lab work, we'd never have got there
without it."

O'Connor turned down the Traffic calls to listen, and made
the obvious comments. And from the time they'd heard
Goulding's report on the bodies they'd known it had to be something like this, but the reality was still a shocking thing.

As Varallo took up the phone to start the machinery going
for that warrant—make it a murder one: you couldn't conceive
any mitigating circumstances on that one—he thought suddenly,
children. Those poor little devils of kids, hardly started in life,
no chance at all, nobody caring—and Rosalie, with people worrying, wondering, every squad car in town looking, just because
she was missing overnight. And just what had got into her,
and why?

Varallo was talking to Louise Fielding on the phone at eleven
o'clock and Wayne was taking a statement from Mrs. Nichols.
O'Connor was listening to the Traffic calls; he'd been home for
a shave and clean shirt and looked somewhat more respectable.
Poor was just sitting there worrying; he felt in his bones that
that lineup the other day had shaken the poor kid some way,
just made it all the more real for her, so that she'd run off in a
panic. At least it was nice weather, and she'd have enough
money on her for food for a day or two.

When his phone light flashed, he just hoped it wasn't a new
call. They had enough to handle right now.

"Oh, Mr. Poor—it's all right, I've got her," said Virginia Waters. "She's O.K."

"You have? Well, thank the Lord. Where was she—how'd you
find her?"

"Well, I know she doesn't have any real close girl friends, and
anyway if she'd gone to a friend the parents would know. She
had told me she just loves the new library, loves to read. So I

just thought I'd look when I had the chance, and there she was, in the main reading room."

"And why the hell did she run?" demanded Poor, belatedly outraged. "Worry her mother half to death, and half the force out looking—"

"Well, she's pretty demoralized right now," said Virginia. "She slept under a tree outside the library, and she didn't take any money with her, she's hungry and dirty and she wants to go home. I haven't asked her any questions. What should I do?"

"Just a minute." Poor relayed that to O'Connor, who let out a blast that was part relief and part annoyance. "Mrs. Keating's at home, I told her she couldn't do anything here. Better have Virginia take her straight there? O.K. . . . Look, you take her home, her mother's there. We'll meet you. I suppose she's all right to talk, answer questions."

"If I read her mother right, she's going to answer questions whether she feels like it or not," said Virginia.

Varallo was off the phone by then, and went along for the ride. They got up to the apartment on Dryden Street, in fact, before Virginia and Rosalie, and Mrs. Keating welcomed them in distractedly; Poor had called her before they left. It was a pleasant apartment, its front windows looking out on a central pool and patio. A minute later Virginia showed up with Rosalie —a pale, rather grimy Rosalie in a soiled and wrinkled dress. "Darling!" said Mrs. Keating. "What on earth *got into you*?"

Rosalie uttered a strangled sob and flung her arms round her mother. "I couldn't—I just couldn't—when I saw him last night —and I couldn't tell because—because—you said you liked him better than Ken—and I couldn't stand it! I just couldn't—"

"Rosalie, darling, what do you mean? Saw who last night? What—"

"*Him.* And I thought I'd just *go*—because—but then I forgot my key and I'd spent all my money on that new purse—" She fumbled for a handkerchief. "You like him! You said you like him—and I just couldn't—see him again—"

Mrs. Keating was looking bewildered. "Do you mean Howie Thurstan? When he came to take me out last night? But, darling—why?"

"Oh-oh-oh!" sobbed Rosalie. "B-because he was the one— did it—and he asked me not to tell and I wouldn't—b-because I thought you were going to m-marry him—but when I saw him again I couldn't—couldn't stand it—"

"Well, for the love of Jesus Christ!" said O'Connor in naked astonishment.

Mrs. Keating said, "Howie? It was Howie Thurstan who— oh, my God! Oh, my God!" She had gone dead white, and she looked at the detectives with eyes suddenly wild. "Howie? That night I was out with Ken? He—"

Rosalie sobbed and hiccuped. "He was sorry—he asked me not to tell—and I didn't, I didn't—when they asked me what the man was like I made up things—like the scar—and I wasn't go- ing to tell, but when you went out with him—and I saw him— I thought how it'd be if you married him—oh-oh-oh!" wailed Rosalie.

Mrs. Keating stood up suddenly, looking to their fascinated eyes like one of the Valkyrie; her dark eyes were flashing and her hands were fists and she spoke in a kind of loud hiss. "Howie Thurstan! You thought—by the good God," she said to O'Con- nor, "I hope you put that man away for a long, long time, Lieutenant—because, by the Lord, if you don't he'd better keep away from us! I'll kill him with my own hands—I'd like to see him boiled in oil—I'd like to see him tortured on the rack! I could—"

"I'd bet," said O'Connor. "But jail will do, if you'll tell us where to find him, Mrs. Keating."

You could say this and that about human nature. They found Howard Thurstan in his office; he had a small insurance agency on Glendale Avenue. He wasn't a bad-looking fellow, about forty, tall and thin, with a receding hairline and the easy extroverted charm of the salesman. But his smile faltered when he saw the badges, and he sank back in his desk chair and slumped forward.

"She told," he said in a muffled voice. "God, I knew she would. God, I don't know what got into me. I must have been crazy."

"You'll have to hear about your rights, Mr. Thurstan," said Varallo.

"I don't care," he said. "Maybe I need a head doctor. Don't know what got into me. Julia Keating's a damn fine woman, I'd—I'd even thought of asking her to marry me—always shied off getting hooked again since the divorce— Goddamn it, I'm not a nut or a queer! I—that night—I'd forgotten Julia said she was tied up, going out—I just went over to see her, ask her out for a drink or something—and—and the kid was there alone. A cute kid, and—not exactly a kid, you know—I don't know what got into me, but all of a sudden—"

"Mr. Thurstan, I hate like hell to tell you," said O'Connor, "but you don't have to tell us anything until you've seen a lawyer. You're under arrest. Come on."

"Oh, my God," said Thurstan, and got up and gave a wild look around the office. "My God—just a minute's impulse—I must have been crazy—and it'll be in the papers—all my clients —my whole life, damn it—"

"You should have thought of that before, Mr. Thurstan," said Poor coldly.

A middle-aged woman came in briskly. "You can go out to lunch now, Mr. Thurstan, I'll get right at that Silcox file."

"He's going somewhere besides to lunch," said Poor.

"And you know," said O'Connor, after they'd booked him in and applied for the warrant and gone out to the place round the corner for lunch, "you know what else this does, don't you?" He eyed his cheeseburger with bitter animosity. "When I think of all the legwork we did on that goddamned description—"

"Oh yes," said Varallo with a sigh. "Yes, indeed, Charles

That description. She's a nice girl, Rosalie. She thought her mother liked Howie, and she wasn't going to tell her what a bad man Howie was. Just a little confused in her loyalties, Rosalie. So when we asked her what the man looked like, she just made up a description as unlike Howie as possible. At least give her some credit, boys."

"On what, for God's sake?" O'Connor attacked the cheese-burger as if it were a mortal enemy.

"She could have picked out one of those unsavory punks and said, He's the one, and we'd have been off on a wilder wild goose chase. Any of them could have been," said Varallo. "We're the ones who tied up Rosalie's rapist with the Maggie Walters nut —she didn't know anything about that, she just said what she thought John wanted to hear. But if she'd identified one of those, we'd have been morally sure we'd caught up to him, even when there wasn't any solid evidence."

"Oh, I see it," said Poor. "But, my God, to think of the rig-marole that kid led us into, all because of some damn fool kid's notion—" He sat back, drank coffee, and after a moment grinned reluctantly. "Well, she is a nice little girl. And her mother's a nice woman. Only I'll bet she'll be a lot more careful about her boy friends in the future."

About two-thirty Duff buzzed Varallo and said, "Your up-state visitors are here." Varallo and O'Connor went downstairs together. In the lobby a big, chesty fellow in natty sports clothes, carrying a wide-brimmed hat that was nearly a Stetson, said, "Varallo? Babcock."

"Glad to meet you. This is Lieutenant O'Connor. You made good time down."

"Not much traffic on a weekday." It was making conversation. "Here are your suspects." He nodded at them. "I haven't said any more to 'em. Just that you've got some questions."

"Very circumspect," said O'Connor, and Babcock looked surprised at the three-syllable word. "You're welcome to sit in. The more witnesses the better."

Mr. and Mrs. William Waldman were not a prepossessing pair. He looked about thirty, with shoulder-length blond hair and a scraggly attempt at a beard. He had on jeans, a garishly printed shirt, and thong sandals on bare feet. Alice Waldman was younger, her brown hair tied back with a frayed ribbon, no make-up except a lot of lipstick; she was chewing gum, and looked bored and mad. She had a good figure, in tight red pants and a white blouse. They sat side by side on the vinyl couch just inside the lobby door, with a battered suitcase between them.

Babcock said without a smile, "I told them they might be staying overnight. He doesn't seem to recall talking to me last night—got the idea you're after them for the back rent they skipped."

"Isn't that fine and dandy," said O'Connor. "Let's surprise them." They took the Waldmans upstairs to the office and gave them chairs. "Before we start, Mr. Waldman, I'd better tell you about your rights," and he recited that to them.

"What do I want a lawyer for?" asked Waldman. "I can't afford no lawyer. Listen, this is a goddamn nuisance. I told that guy I'd pay up the rent when I got some bread. Anyways it was only a month. Besides, the damn place wasn't worth it—the stove didn't work and you could spit through the walls—"

"Is that so?" said O'Connor. "You had to have a stove to feed the kids, didn't you? Two little boys and the baby. Only you didn't remember to feed them very often, did you? Where are they, Waldman? Do you know, Mrs. Waldman?"

"The kids?" said Waldman. "Uh—they're with Alice's sister."

"No, they're not, Waldman," said Varallo gently. "You know they're not. Is that what he told you, Mrs. Waldman?"

"Oh sure," she said quickly. "That's where they are—aren't they, Bill?" She looked at Varallo guilelessly. There was a moment's silence.

"Did you really believe that, Mrs. Waldman? That your sister would take them?" She shrugged and said nothing.

"Why did you want to get rid of the kids, Waldman?" asked O'Connor.

After a moment Waldman said, "I thought this was about the rent. What the hell, about the kids? We just thought we'd take off without 'em awhile. There isn't no law about it."

"But there is, if you neglect your responsibility," said Varallo, and thought Waldman wouldn't know what the word meant. "Where are they, Waldman? Two little boys—what are their names, by the way? We haven't heard that."

"Oh—Jim and Jacky," said Mrs. Waldman. She put her gum in O'Connor's ashtray and got out a cigarette.

"And the baby—what's the baby's name?"

"Uh—Alicia."

"Where are they, Waldman? You know and we know. Suppose you tell us how they got there."

"I don't know what you mean," said Waldman. "We gotta right to do what we want with our own kids."

"Only up to a point," said O'Connor hardly. "Tell us, Waldman."

"Oh, for God's sake," said Alice Waldman. "Tell them and get it over. There's no law. Listen, people are s'posed to like kids, but there's no law about that either. They were a damn nuisance, always hangin' round wanting things—it was a drag, with the kids. Whinin' around asking alla time—we just decided to get shut of them." They all stared at her. She flicked ash off her cigarette. "Some people like kids and some don't, that's all. If we wasn't married, I coulda got the welfare for 'em, but we couldn't even get that."

"Mrs. Waldman, do you understand what you're saying?" asked O'Connor carefully.

"Sure. There's a place like the welfare, you can take kids to be adopted. Bill took them there, that's all."

Varallo let out a breath. "That's what he told you, is it? What about it, Waldman? Why didn't you take them there? At least give them a chance?"

Waldman looked exasperated, and then he began to look frightened, as it slowly dawned on him that this was all about the kids, that the lawmen knew about that. "For God's sake," he said. "I did—and that dame told me I couldn't just leave 'em —there had to be some kind of talk about it, and somebody come see Alice—and, see, we had tickets for the ice show that night. I didn't know what to do. I left the kids in the car and when I come back they was yelling—" He was silent for a long dragging minute and then he said, "I didn't think—nobody'd ever find them up there."

His wife stared at him. "Didn't you leave them at that welfare place?"

"No, Mrs. Waldman," said O'Connor. "He cut the boys' throats and bashed in the baby's head and he left them up in the hills for the coyotes. Only not far enough up. Would you like to see the pictures we took, how they looked when we found them?"

She uttered a strangled sound. "Well, my God, Alice," said Waldman, goaded, "I didn't know what to do! You said get shut of them, you'd had it with the damn kids, and that dame said about a social worker and coming to see the house and talk to you and all, and I knew you'd be mad! You were gettin' all gussied up to go to the ice show—and when I come back to the car the damn kids was yellin' and the baby was all wet and, hell, I just—I didn't figure anybody'd ever find 'em up there."

The easiest thing to do, thought Varallo, bemused. The expedient thing to do. "How did you come to pick that spot, Mr. Waldman?" he asked.

"Huh? Oh, I didn't, exactly—I was just drivin' around, and it looked pretty wild up there. It was lucky the blood was mostly on the seat covers, but I shoulda thought—I took those off."

"My God, Bill!" said his wife. "My God!" She put out her cigarette. "You goddamned fool! You didn't need to do a crazy thing like that! You coulda just left 'em on the street somewhere, the welfare woulda took 'em!"

"Come to the big city and see life," said Varallo.

"Oh, we get some in the sticks too," said Babcock with a tight smile. "You've got a nice little plant here."

"You should see LAPD. We don't compare. We're much obliged for the help."

"I should hope so," said Babcock. "The riffraff is riffraff wherever. Is there any place around I can get a good steak?" Varallo recommended Damon's. "Fine. Think I'll pick up an early dinner and head back to the wilds. Any day, Varallo, I'll take my beat rather than yours."

It was four-thirty, with an hour and a half of the shift to go. When Varallo got back upstairs, O'Connor was back from booking the Waldmans in. There really wasn't anything to say about the Waldmans, but Poor was on the phone telling Goulding all about it. Forbes was hunched over his typewriter, and looked up as Varallo came in.

"I've just got some more names from the phone company on these Narco clients of Esteban's. They've got to be followed up sometime—I could use some help."

There were no leads, of course, on the two latest heists, no descriptions. They had sent off a query to Chicago about the Harris woman; possibly something in her pedigree with Chicago would suggest something useful; it wasn't too likely, but they had to try. The A.P.B. was still out on that hit-run.

Reluctantly O'Connor approached his typewriter, hunted out carbon, and rolled in the 510 form for a first report on the Waldmans. Out of the corner of his eye Varallo watched him amusedly. O'Connor hated that typewriter; it was a diabolical machine he coped with by main strength. This time he got a reprieve. His phone light flashed on, and a moment later he sprang up, feeling automatically for the shoulder holster.

"Vic—our female heisters—a chance we'll catch up to them, by God! That was the guy from the liquor store, he just spotted them going into a dress shop up on Kenneth—"

# TEN

They fell into O'Connor's Ford in the lot. "Said he was just coming to take over the night shift," said O'Connor tersely, and cussed at getting the red light as he swung onto Wilson. "Recognized them right off—they're even wearing the same clothes, he said, and of all the gall—"

It was five blocks over to Brand, fourteen up to Kenneth, eight to Grandview, and O'Connor made record time. There was a green-painted parking slot opposite the drugstore, and he stepped on the parking brake and jerked out the ignition key in one motion; they were out and heading up toward the dress shop in the middle of the block the next second.

The big gray-haired fellow, Chris from the liquor store, was lingering in front of the gift shop next door. "They're still in there," he greeted them excitedly, "I think they're still there—of all the damned nerve, come right back to the same neighborhood! I hope Miss Yates is O.K., she doesn't usually close till six, but the CLOSED sign was up when I came back from phoning you—"

O'Connor used his key ring to beat a brisk tattoo on the glass door. "Is there a rear door?" asked Varallo.

Chris shook his head. "Nope. Wonder the fire department hasn't said anything—no rear doors along here at all."

"Police!" shouted O'Connor. "Open up!" A couple of men thrust startled heads from the barber shop next to the gift shop. The glass door was tinted, and the window was obscured with life-size models displaying clothes, but they could discern some startled movement in there, a flurry of struggle, and suddenly a woman fell against the door inside, a bolt snapped, and she fell out at them.

"Help!" she gasped feebly. "Help—police—save me!" She was a thin, elderly woman with a halo of wild white hair. "They've got a gun!"

"Stay back!" snapped O'Connor. He had the .357 magnum out, and Varallo his Police Positive. They ran into the store and the first thing they saw was the baby, a plump, clean, blond baby contentedly cuddling a diminutive teddy bear, in the middle of the floor. At the back of the store, a leggy blonde had just stepped out of a fitting room, buttoning a dress. She stared at them, frozen, and let out a wail.

"Myrna, she got out! There's men—"

Another young woman appeared out of a second fitting room. She was simply clad in briefs and a bra, and had a pile of dresses and pants over one arm. "Oh hell!" she said.

"You're both under arrest!" said O'Connor. "We're police, and you've been identified. Vic, have a look for the gun."

"Of all the damned lousy luck!" said the brunette disgustedly.

"I told you we shouldn't come back here," said the blonde.

"But I saw that pantsuit in the window—oh, for God's sake!" said the brunette. "The gun's in my purse there, we wouldn't have shot anybody. Of all the lousy luck!"

Varallo put his gun away and opened the shabby white handbag on the counter. The gun was a Colt .32, in good condition, and quite empty. "Suppose we hear your names," he suggested. "Er—and you'd better get dressed, Miss—"

"Mrs. Mrs. Myrna Lloyd," she said. "And this is Betty Jean Schirmer." The blonde let out a little wail. "Oh, shut up, Betty —they got us, there's no use screaming about it. I better put something on."

The baby started to cry and Betty Jean rushed over to it. "We weren't after any *money* here," she said to O'Connor earnestly. "Just the clothes—for Hawaii, you know—they've got some awfully smart things here. There, darling, Mommy's here. Oh, my goodness, but Dick's going to be mad! Oooh, won't he be mad!"

By the time the brunette was dressed and they got them out to the car, there was a crowd of curious witnesses from the drugstore, the barber shop, the gift shop, the bakery across the street. Miss Yates was agitatedly recounting her experience to Kogan beside the black-and-white; dispatched by Duff, he'd got held up in a jam on Glenoaks. "And what about Myrna's car? Where are you taking us? Can I call my husband?"

At the station, the two sat side by side in front of O'Connor's desk, the blonde a little scared, the brunette more annoyed. They had both had identification in their handbags: Mrs. Myrna Lloyd, Mrs. Richard Schirmer, of next-door addresses on Milford Street. "Would you like to tell us about this?" said O'Connor after he'd read them the piece about their rights.

"Well, I guess it sort of went further than we meant," said Betty Jean mournfully. "I mean, everything's been getting so expensive. Myrna's divorced and only got the part-time job—we just got to be friends when she moved next door—and Dick—my husband—he's a bus driver for the city, and he's awfully good, he gives me what he can but it isn't so much. With the prices and all. And we were watching TV one night—Myrna and me, I mean, Dick was working—and I said to Myrna, it looks like a sort of easy way to get some money. If we only had a gun."

"And so I went and got a gun at a pawnshop," said Myrna. "It wasn't loaded, I don't know anything about guns. We just thought at first, take enough to make it a little easier, all the grocery bills and the electric bills and the rent—"

"But they all just handed it over so *easy*," said Betty Jean. "All that nice money! It was just like a dream. More than I'd ever seen—and we decided to get enough for a trip to Hawaii. We'd tell Dick that Myrna won the tickets in a contest, and he wouldn't have minded my going. Now I guess we don't get to go, and we had almost enough."

"Jail instead," said Myrna gloomily. "Well, it'll be a new experience. And at least there won't be any grocery bills. Could I bum a cigarette from somebody?" Varallo gave her one and lit it. "Thanks. I guess we were crazy to try it, but it was nice while it lasted."

Betty Jean wiped her eyes and sat back, and a slow dreamy smile spread on her face. "I never had so much fun in my life," she said. "All that lovely, lovely money. I got Dick that camera he wanted for his birthday, and all the pretty clothes for the baby, and just lots I'd always wanted—I never had so much fun."

"Would you like to call your husband now, Mrs. Schirmer?" O'Connor's mouth was twitching.

"I guess I'd better. Oh, he's going to be mad!" said Betty Jean.

It was Rhys's night off, and Hunter was on night watch alone. He sat playing solitaire, bored, and no calls came in at all until midnight. Then he got a call to an assault over on Portola Avenue.

When he got there the lights were on in back and front—it was a single house—and Gordon was waiting by the black-and-white in front. "I had a good look around, but he's long gone. She's a Mrs. Sturgess, Mary Sturgess."

"O.K.," said Hunter, and went up to the porch. As he listened to Mrs. Sturgess, he started wondering whether they might have something here.

"What he didn't know was," said Mrs. Sturgess gaily, "that I'm an insomniac. If I'd been asleep I don't suppose I'd have heard him, but I was awake and I did. My son's been telling me we ought to get a better lock on that back door. I heard it go, with just a loud crack, and I heard a man come into the kitchen. My son always says I've got no nerves at all, and I can't say I was frightened, I just slipped out to the hall and got the baseball bat—"

"Er—your son doesn't live with you?" asked Hunter. She didn't look over thirty.

She laughed. "Oh, yes, but he's away at summer camp—with

the Boy Scouts—and my husband's in Fresno for the company. I'd got the bat for Bobby's birthday next week, it was in the hall closet, and it was the first handy weapon I thought of. I just waited, and when I heard him come into the hall, I just batted him. As hard as I could."

"Did you hit him, you think?"

"Oh, I think so—only not his head," she said regretfully. "He made a funny kind of sound, and then he *whispered* at me —of all things—he said, why'd you do that, lady—and he started to run out again, and I chased him to the back door, and he grabbed the bat and nearly got it away from me, and then he ran out the kitchen door."

"Whispered at you?" said Hunter. "And when he got in, he started right for the bedrooms?" It just could be, he thought, that that had been their rapist, having bad luck the second time in a row. "Excuse me, Mrs. Sturgess, didn't you think to switch on a light? To get a look at him?"

"Oh, I thought of that afterward," she said brightly. "No nerves, but no sense either, I expect Bobby'll say. The switch was right beside me in the hall, but I just never thought of it— that would have surprised him even more than the baseball bat, wouldn't it?"

Repressing any comment, Hunter went to look for the bat. It was lying beside the kitchen door. "Did you touch this again, ma'am? You had hold of it at the bottom?" It was just possible that X had left some prints on it; it was worth a try anyway. He went out to the car for an evidence bag and nudged the bat into it, for transportation to the lab. "Could we ask you to come in tomorrow to let us take your fingerprints, Mrs. Sturgess? Just for comparison, if we find any others on this."

"Why, I'd love to," she said. "Won't that be something to tell Bobby!"

Hunter's report was waiting on Saturday morning, and O'Connor was convinced that that had been their boy, just on the evidence of the whispering. "Is he losing his touch, or just unlucky the last couple of tries? And there you are—he cases these women enough, somehow, to know when they're alone."

"Could be just an ordinary burglar who's picked up the flu and lost his voice," said Katz disparagingly. "Nothing really says that was him."

"Well, we'll see if he left any prints on that bat," said O'Connor.

Robert Finch came in, a gray and ravaged man, to sign a statement, and Katz talked to him. A new burglary went down just then, a small appliance store on Colorado, and Wayne and Poor went out on that. When Finch left, Katz was stymied on his narco jobs because the phone company was still tracking down more names for him. He was just typing an interim report on it when Traffic caught up to that A.P.B. on the hit-run and fetched him in, and Varallo sat in on that questioning. They booked him in and went out to lunch, where O'Connor joined them ten minutes later.

"Telex in from Chicago," he said, passing it across the table to Varallo, "and it says damn all. This Harris is just a common tart with the run-of-the-mill record for a tart, and nobody's heard of her for five years. Just like I said, she could be anywhere in L. A. County, and where the hell and how the hell Loomis ran across her—of all the unlikely pairs!"

There just wasn't any way to start looking for Harris.

They'd just got back to the office when O'Connor took a call from Patrolman Tracy, who had a body to report. "Off a horse," he said. "I'm up here—"

"Off a what? What the hell are you talking about?"

"He got thrown off a horse, sir. I'm up here in the annex, just below Dunsmore Canyon on New York. The horse was running away down New York, so it's in our territory. I've called an ambulance, but he's dead all right."

"A horse!" said O'Connor. But at the moment they were at loose ends, and he and Varallo went up there to look at it.

Neither of them had been up that way since that night a year and a half ago when they'd all been out hunting the two lost little girls. They both remembered that vividly, but they didn't talk about it as they drove up New York Street to where the black-and-white waited.

The body was in the street, a man about thirty-five, in a natty western outfit complete with cowboy boots and a Stetson. The ambulance had just got there. The horse, a handsome palomino, was quietly cropping grass in somebody's front yard, and it looked as if everybody on the street and all the kids and dogs in the Glendale annex had come out to watch.

"Fell off and landed on his head," said one of the ambulance attendants, bending over the body.

"Does anybody know who he is?" asked O'Connor.

"Yes, sir. That is, they know the horse," said Tracy. "It's from a stable back in the hills up the canyon, a couple of the people along here had seen him riding it before, and I called up there—the owner of the stable said—"

Varallo remembered him the minute he showed up, though he hadn't thought of him from that day to this: a wiry fellow named Dick Pool, who had helped them on that long hunt, that clear starry night. He came down on another horse, and swung off in a hurry, seeing the crowd.

"So the damn fool finally killed himself," he said in disgust. He went and collected the palomino expertly, dragging the reins over its head. "God knows it's not the horse's fault."

"Who is he, Mr. Pool?"

"Sanford Ziegler," said Pool. "He lives over on Boston, you'll have to call his wife. The poor silly bastard—more money than sense. You know what his lifelong ambition was? He wanted to ride in the Rose Parade on New Year's. On a fancy horse, with a fancy western outfit and fancy gear and all. The damn fool'd never been on a horse in his life up to three months ago, but as soon as he's got the money he goes and buys this nice fellow here"—Pool patted the palomino's neck—"and stables him with me. I told him, Mr. Ziegler, I said, that's a horse for an experienced rider—there's no vice in him, but he's young and frisky and he likes to run—you ought to start out on some quiet old nag, I said. But does he listen? Not on your life. Every time he climbs aboard, naturally the horse knows he's got no control at all, and if he fell off once he was off him regular as clockwork every time he tried to ride him. His wife told him, I told him, the stablehands told him, but he wouldn't listen. You see what comes of it. You just remember to put in your report, it wasn't the horse's fault." With a snort Pool swung back on his own horse and started back up the hill, leading the palomino.

"Lot of fools in the world," said the ambulance attendant.

"So now we have to go and break the bad news to his wife," said O'Connor, annoyed.

They climbed the stairs to the office and just as they got to the door, Katz let out a muffled yell. He was sitting at his desk holding the phone. "What's that again? I don't believe it. Spell it. Well, I will be good and goddamned! No, sweetheart, I'm not cussing you—thanks." He put down the phone and, noticing O'Connor and Varallo, crooked a finger at them. "Come here and look at this. You won't believe it either, and it's another very funny damned thing. That was the phone company, with the last batch of names and addresses for us on these narco clients. And you'll never guess who just showed up on it. Look." He stabbed a finger at his own hasty scrawl, the last name he'd put down.

*Carole Mederos, 1401 Kenilworth.*

"Well, I'll be damned," said O'Connor. "that's a funny one all right, Joe. That girl in Loomis' office—"

"And wouldn't C. P. Adrian have seven fits," said Varallo. "Don't we know, the casual use up, even with the nominally respectable working people—but that girl—I don't know, this rocks me." Katz reached for the sheet but he hung onto it, studying it. "Damn it, that girl—butter not melting in her mouth. Strictly from Boresville, she said—and that was God's truth, until we found Loomis was human like everybody else—Look, Charles, all these names have to be followed up sooner or later. Come on, let's go see Carole and find out if she's holding. Saturday afternoon, she might be home."

"Waste time on a petty charge," grumbled O'Connor, but he came. It was just funny enough to arouse their curiosity.

The address on Kenilworth was a big apartment house, not out of line in probable rent for what the Mederos girl would be earning. There wasn't any pool or patio; they looked at mailboxes, and found her listed in 420. There was a self-service elevator and they rode up in it.

"She didn't strike me as the type," said O'Connor, "but is there a type?"

As they walked down the hall toward 420, they could hear a stereo going, subdued out here, on *Rhapsody in Blue*. It was evidently in 420. Varallo pushed the bell. After a moment he pushed it again. The door began to open and the music swelled out.

"Harry, you're late—what the hell?" said Carole Mederos. She stared at Varallo and O'Connor. But they were looking past her into the apartment.

"Well, well," said O'Connor. "Old home week, I see." Most of them were there, the daily toilers at C. P. Adrian Tax Agency. Jim Dumbarton, frozen with a glass in his hand. Adam Secrist in the act of kissing Paula Fearn's neck as she squealed and giggled. Steve O'Dell and Lynn Newman cozied up on the couch. "Can we join the party?"

"What the hell do you want?" said Carole. "That's all it is, just a party. It's Jim's birthday."

"And you bought him a fresh supply of the grass? Or was it speed or H you were buying from Roddy Esteban?" asked Varallo interestedly.

She stood motionless one moment, and then she screamed, "You go straight to hell!" and flung her glass in his face. He dodged quickly, and the glass smashed on the wall behind him, the liquor splattering over his shoulders.

"Now I don't call that a very friendly gesture," drawled O'Connor, and reached for her; but Varallo forestalled him.

As she stepped back, he caught her by the shoulders, and then with both hands swept all the dark hair back from her face, covering it roughly. *"Per l'amore di Dio!"* he said. "Look—quick, Charles!" She pulled away and turned her back. "But what blind idiots we were not to see it! A good dye job, different make-up, and a new name—"

"My Christ!" said O'Connor.

"But you've still got the same prints, Elizabeth Ann," said Varallo. "And still the same hot temper, don't you? Was that what you said to Loomis just before you tossed that bookend at him?"

She stood like a statue, but the rest of the tableau broke up in confusion and noise.

"You're all coming," said O'Connor into the babel, "until we make some sense out of this!"

One thing to be said for her, she'd dealt with cops before and knew all the routine; she knew they had her prints, and there was no point in trying to back out of it. She'd lost a gamble, and she sat beside O'Connor's desk and told them what they asked, flat and hard.

"I got out and made something of myself, five years back—you can see that. I started using my mother's maiden name, I went to business school and came out here and got a decent job. I've been clean—that way—ever since. And it was Lynn wanted to try the dope first," she added bitterly. Now that their eyes were open, they could see the resemblance to that mug shot: the face shape, the set of the eyes.

"At your little office parties?" said Varallo. "And how long has that been going on?"

She shrugged. "Life's a drag—you have fun where you can, don't you? Jim Dumbarton's fed up with his wife and Steve's divorced—Adam isn't married, and what the hell business was it of anybody's, we get together to have a little fun? But we knew how the boss would take it, it was strictly private—my place or Lynn's, sometimes. Sally doesn't know about it—she's a nice kid."

"All right. So Lynn—or somebody—thought it'd add a few kicks to try the pot or speed, or something. We'll find out. And you found a supplier."

"I knew the route to look," she agreed shortly.

"And how did Loomis find out?"

"Oh, my God, that—that old maid! What the hell business was it of his or anybody else's? That Friday, I'd met Esteban on my lunch hour and picked up some stuff. Speed—you'll find some of it left, in the apartment. I don't use the stuff—I get a better high on a few drinks—but Harry and Adam liked the speed because it's a quick high and doesn't show. One thing about a tax agency, Harry said, he could always tell his wife he was working overtime on somebody's deductions. Well, anyway. I was just coming into the office when I ran into Mr. Do-Right Loomis and dropped my damn bag, and everything fell out, and he saw the stuff—"

"I wouldn't have thought he'd have recognized what it was," said O'Connor.

"Well, damn it, it was labeled—I was in a hurry, I just met Esteban over by the public library and paid him and shoved it in my bag—a little box, labeled METH. I guess there's been enough in the papers about users, anybody'd know what that was. And dear Mr. Loomis—oh, he was such a noble guy!— he called me up to his desk later on and delivered the little lecture. Not to embarrass me in front of anybody, he said. But he felt it was his duty to tell Mr. Adrian—we used to call it snitching when I was in P.S. 138 back in Chicago. He said it was a very serious thing, I'd be making mistakes, taking such stuff, and we had a responsibility to the firm. And he'd give me the weekend to think it over, and if I promised him I'd give it up he'd give me a second chance. *He'd* give me—! Just who told him he was God Almighty to say that to anybody? But I could see what a mess it was going to be. It wouldn't make any difference if I said to him on Monday, sure, I'll be a good girl, please don't tell the boss. He would have anyway. He was that kind."

"And you'd have got fired," said Varallo.

She turned to him quickly. "It wasn't just that! I knew the minute that happened, that damn fool Jim would go to Adrian and say it wasn't my fault, they'd asked me to get the stuff—and it'd all have come out, and everybody'd have got fired."

"Which he'd have known, so he'd have kept his mouth shut," said O'Connor.

"You don't know Jim. He'd never have thought of that, just rushed into the boss to get me off the hook. He's a damn fool. His wife's going to divorce him, and he wants me to marry him, but—even before all this—I've got better sense than that. He's too nice a guy to get stuck with me."

"I see," said Varallo. "So what did you do?"

"I went to see Loomis that night. I thought if I told him I was going to quit the job, just ask him not to say anything, let me get out— That way, I could've convinced Jim I just wanted a different job or something, and it'd have been all right. You can bet the rest of them would have kept quiet, if that had come out! But dear Mr. Loomis—Mr. High and Mighty Loomis —gave me such a nice lecture on the evils of drugs and what awful things it would lead to, I—damn it, I lost my temper, that's all."

Varallo laughed. "Grabbed up that bookend and threw it, and ran out. And the door slammed and locked."

"I thought it was lucky I'd hung onto my purse, or you'd have found it there and known right off. I never thought about fingerprints, then. And I never knew—he was dead—till you showed up that Wednesday. I just didn't know what to think when he didn't come into the office, I just kept quiet, didn't say anything to Jim or any of them. If Mr. Adrian had realized he wasn't there, he'd have checked up right away, but he didn't.

And I guess all the rest of them were waiting to see how long he'd play hooky, and what Adrian'd do when he found out."

"And then we turned up and told you he was dead." Varallo looked at O'Connor. In a way you could respect Elizabeth Ann Harris; she had come a rough road, and in her own way she was a straight shooter.

O'Connor got on the phone about the warrant, and Varallo took her over and booked her in. It was going to be a mess anyway, the rest of them all held on the holding charge, and probably C. P. Adrian was going to have a heart attack when he found out. He'd be left with just that nice kid, Sally, in his tax agency.

It was nearly six o'clock, and Varallo only went back to the office to kick it around a little before going home. Burt was just coming out of the lab. "There were some dandy latents on that baseball bat," he said. "Not Mrs. Sturgess'. They're not in our files. I sent 'em to LAPD and Washington."

"Good," said Varallo absently.

On Sunday morning O'Connor took Maisie up into that canyon above New York street; he'd forgotten about that wild piece of land up there, a fine place for her to gallop around. He left the car down about where that body had been, and toiled up the rough trail after her. Long legs flashing, ears and topknot flying, Maisie covered a lot of ground above and around him.

Down from that stable and riding ring up there, some horses were loose in a fenced field, and Maisie flirted over the fence to greet some new friends. O'Connor leaned on the fence and lit a cigarette.

"Hey!" said an outraged voice. "Hey, you get that mutt out of there!" O'Connor looked up to face Dick Pool, on a horse. "Is that your mutt?"

"She's not a—"

"Well, you get it out of there! It's spooking those nags to hell and back!"

The horses were certainly running around like mad, with

Maisie capering after them happily. O'Connor went after her with the leash. Possibly he ought to make the effort, as Mary Lou McNally said, to get to that obedience training.

Katharine and Laura went up to Pike's Verdugo Oaks, to sample the delightful Sunday brunch. "Though I must say," said Katharine, helping herself liberally to crab salad, "nobody can touch the salad dressing at Damon's."

"I thought once it'd be worth the effort of getting a job as cook there, to learn the secret," agreed Laura, piling her plate with shrimp Newburgh. "How did the cradle turn out?"

"Oh, lovely. I used that new antiquing kit from Kaufman's and it came out beautifully. I do love the way they stuff celery here," said Katharine.

"And all the different rolls." Laura caught a waiter's eye and asked for more butter. "You know, Katharine, we're going to have to cut down. Twenty pounds, the doctor said, and I've gained seventeen already."

"Next week," said Katharine. "I know, I've gained eighteen. But I'm not going to worry about it now. Next week, we'll stop."

On Monday morning, the first call they had was from the Brand Library: vandalism overnight. That was technically part of the public library, but it was the old Brand Castle up on the hill, the extensive grounds now made into a big park, and the library kept all its art work, records and tapes there. Varallo went up to look, and it was a monumental mess. The vandals had got in through a skylight, and smashed records, slashed pictures, thrown paint around, demolished office machines and tape recorders. He called back to the station for Burt or Thomsen; it wasn't very likely the vandals had left any prints, but there might be other physical evidence to pick up.

The paperwork was still going on, on the anonymous heisters, on the latest burglary, on Katz's narco list. The warrants were in on Fielding, on Thurstan, on Myrna and Betty Jean. They'd had

Betty Jean's husband in yesterday, a bewildered and angry young man. His mother was looking after the baby.

At ten o'clock the routine kickback came in from the Feds: the prints on that baseball bat. And O'Connor, casually glancing over the Telex, suddenly let out a roar. "By God, here he is! We've got him! I don't believe it, but we've got him!" He waved the Telex at Varallo.

The prints belonged to Ronald Edward Ames, convicted of the rape of Janice Walters five years ago in Smith City, California. "Where the hell is Smith City?" asked O'Connor, and scrabbled in the atlas.

"What do you mean, we've got him?" said Varallo. "*Janice* Walters? What the hell does this say?"

"Let's find out!" said O'Connor energetically. "Here it is!—it's a wide place in the road just this side of the Oregon border. I wonder if there's a police force." He used the phone and eventually reached somebody who said he was the Chief of Police. His name was Percy. O'Connor remembered to put the phone on the amplifier; they were all standing around, interested.

"Ronnie Ames?" said Chief Percy. He sounded elderly and a little slow. "Don't tell me he's in any trouble down there—did you say lieutenant? Police? I'd sure be sorry to hear that."

"Well, we don't know. The record says he was convicted of rape up there."

"That's right, but I never thought Ronnie did that. That Maggie Walters—folks always called her Maggie, her other name's Margaret, on account her ma was named Janice too— she didn't have too good a reputation, you take me, and if you ask me she just needed an excuse on account of the baby. But Ronnie, he's kind of a loner, and he never had too many good friends like, even in school. Folks seemed to think he was a little off, because he had some kind of sickness when he was a baby and can't talk no more than a whisper, like. But Ronnie's all right, I always thought, just kind of shy. Only the jury listened to Maggie, and—"

O'Connor cut him short. "All we want to know is, do you

know where he is now? He served a sentence for it—he's out, and
down here somewhere?"

"Oh, yeah. He got out last year. Is he in any trouble down
there? I'd be sorry to hear that. He always struck me as a nice
enough young fellow. Yeah, he got out of Vacaville, oh, last fall,
I guess—his mother still lives here, you know, nice woman—and
I guess he thought, best not to come back here, he went to live
with his sister—did you say you're talking from Glendale? California? Well, that's where she lives, his sister—she married a fellow from Klamath—"

"What's her name?" barked O'Connor.

"Well, now, I'd have to stop and think. Her mother'd know,
of course. It was a foreign name, I seem to recollect," said Percy,
"and he was a Catholic, I know there was some talk about it, because the Ameses are strict Methodist—"

"Can you call her mother and find out the name, please?"

"But she was a nice girl. I suppose they thought, give Ronnie
a better start in another place—he was only twenty-one when he
got convicted—Martinez," said Percy. "That was it. She married
a fellow named John Martinez."

O'Connor let out a despairing grunt. "Martinez! My God,
how many in the phone book?"

They found him on the sixteenth try, a John Martinez who
worked for the gas company and owned a house on Doran
Street. They found Ronald Ames, who was a mild-looking little
fellow, and who admitted readily enough he'd been the one who
raped those women.

"I never did it to Maggie," he whispered. "But everybody said
I did. I thought—I just thought I would do it—to get back at
Maggie, like."

He'd found out about the women being alone, he said, on
his job. He had a part-time job trying to sell lots at Forest Lawn.
Sometimes he went door to door, sometimes he used the phone.
He had a beat-up old car. Eventually they would ask, and Stephanie Calvert, Della Espinoza, the other women last January

would vaguely remember the door-to-door salesman, the questions about any family. He was a little man nobody would ever be afraid of.

"And praise the Lord that is cleaned up!" said O'Connor. They now had another burglary, another heist at a liquor store last night, and of course there was no lead on the vandals at all. "When I think what a quiet town this used to be—!"

When Varallo got home that Tuesday night it was still light: daylight saving. He detoured from the garage to admire the beautiful single bloom Pedrálbes had finally achieved: a pure and lovely chartreuse, really something to see. And he seemed to have got to the aphids in time.

In the kitchen, there were pots simmering on the stove, but Laura wasn't there, or in the living room. He went looking, and found her in the nursery, sitting in the rocker over the Dictionary of English Christian Names. Their best baby Ginevra was occupied with the stuffed gray cat, and Gideon Algernon Cadwallader was playing watch-cat on the foot of the bed.

"And why aren't you getting my dinner ready?" Varallo bent to kiss her.

"Oh, Vic—I didn't hear you come in. Dinner'll be ready in a while," said Laura absently. "And I've decided to be a nice meek obedient spouse—I see it's no use arguing at you. If it's a boy it'll be John. So tame and ordinary. But if it should be a girl I've quite decided on Francesca. It'd go with any last name, and it's cute. I like it."

"*Benissimo!*" said Varallo. "I'll just hold the firm thought that it's a boy!"